About the Author

Hi, I am William Gatton, most everyone knows me as Eddie Gatton. I am a fifty-one-year-old electrician from a rural community in Olin, North Carolina, a few miles north of Statesville N.C. I have always loved books; I love reading them and getting lost in another world. A few years ago, I got my first Audible account where I could listen to the books. Wow I am addicted. Anyway, reading all those horror books they inspired me to open up my own imagination and out tumbled *Crazy Eddie's Tales of Horror*.

Crazy Eddie's Tales of Horror

Eddie Gatton

Crazy Eddie's Tales of Horror

Olympia Publishers
London

www.olympiapublishers.com
OLYMPIA PAPERBACK EDITION

Copyright © Eddie Gatton 2022

The right of Eddie Gatton to be identified as author of
this work has been asserted in accordance with sections 77 and 78 of
the Copyright, Designs and Patents Act 1988.

All Rights Reserved

No reproduction, copy or transmission of this publication
may be made without written permission.
No paragraph of this publication may be reproduced,
copied or transmitted save with the written permission of the publisher,
or in accordance with the provisions
of the Copyright Act 1956 (as amended).

Any person who commits any unauthorised act in relation to
this publication may be liable to criminal
prosecution and civil claims for damage.

A CIP catalogue record for this title is
available from the British Library.

ISBN: 978-1-80074-208-6

This is a work of fiction.
Names, characters, places and incidents originate from the writer's
imagination. Any resemblance to actual persons, living or dead, is
purely coincidental.

First Published in 2022

Olympia Publishers
Tallis House
2 Tallis Street
London
EC4Y 0AB

Printed in Great Britain

Dedication

Dedicated to my wife, Lisa, for her patience and encouragement throughout this crazy ride.

Acknowledgements

I would like to thank all the wonderful folks at Olympia Publishing for believing in me. I would also like to thank all the family and friends that believed I could do it.
Hey, I did it!

THE TRIP

Here we have Amanda Goodson, a strong-willed widow who lost her husband in a plane crash ten years ago. She has been a spastic overprotective mother for her son Jason ever since the crash. She has limited him to school and the home to keep him safe. Amanda has tried to keep her son Jason safe by protecting him from the cruelty of the world. So, she imagined. We now have Jason Goodson, who lost his father in the plane crash when he was eight years old. Jason is a super smart young man. He has just graduated from high school at the top of his class. Despite the chaotic childhood he has had with his overprotective mother. Amanda Goodson's simple cozy world was suddenly flung into the eye of a hurricane. From which life will soon fall from existence.

The phone rang at 9:30 am at the Goodson house. Amanda Goodson walked from the kitchen to the living room only to snatch up the receiver on the third ring.

'Hello Goodson residence.'

'Hello, Mrs Goodson, I am John Houston, CEO of Form-a-cell.'

At the mention of his name there came a small giggle that Amanda tried to suppress with great difficulty, but she could not contain the giggle. 'Yes, how may I help you? Mr. Houston.'

'I called to speak with Jason Goodson.

With the giggle still trying to burst out into a full-blown case of laughter. She said please hold the line. I will go upstairs and fetch him for you.

Amanda sat the phone receiver down on the small table attached to the gossip bench, as Mr Goodson had called it. She started for the stairs of the small cottage that she and her son have shared for the last ten years. As she made her way up the stairs the remembrance of the movie quote ran through her mind again. 'Houston, we have a problem.' from that movie with Tom Hanks in it. Amanda reached the top of the stairs just as Jason came out of his room. She was still giggling a little as he saw his mom. Amanda startled to a full halt at his sudden appearance as she gasped in surprise. 'There is a Mr Houston on the phone for you,' with a loud yell.

'Yes,' and a pumping motion of his hands. Jason was glowing with excitement. 'It must be the man about the job.'

'Job?' his mother asked with alarm. 'What job?' his mother asked with a lot of concern in her voice. 'When did you apply for a job?'

Jason never responded to her questions as he bounded down the stairs two at a time, stopping at the bottom to calm his breath.

Amanda was in shock, her mind was racing in a whirlwind of questions. She started back down the stairway in slow motion steps. A job, he has just graduated from high school two months ago. As she made her way to sit on the bottom step. Her whole intention for this was to eavesdrop on Jason's phone call with Mr. Houston. 'Houston, we have a major problem here,' My son has said nothing about getting a job before now.

Amanda could only hear one side of the conversation. 'Hello Mr Houston, yes this is Jason Goodson, yes, sir.' A brief pause, with Jason nodding his head yes, before answering, 'Yes, sir.' to the phone. Another brief pause, 'Yes, sir, I have a 2006 Land Rover. It was a graduation gift from my mother.'

Another two longer pauses then he said, 'yes, sir, I see, what? California? Why yes, sir, I can be there by the first of next week.'

At this statement, Amanda Goodson's heart sank into the pit of her stomach. She shook her head, 'no' as these thoughts flooded her mind. I cannot lose Jason too. Amanda had lost her husband ten years ago in a plane crash. She had taken the settlement money and bought this little cottage for her and Jason to live out their lives together. He cannot leave me; he is all I have left in this cruel world. There were two more rounds of 'yes, sirs,' but Amanda did not notice. She was losing her mind to the world in thought.

Jason's mom snapped back into reality when Jason placed his hands onto her shoulder. She jumped in surprise. She looked up into Jason's face. Everything she blurted out through the sobs, which were coming on with a vengeance.

'You cannot leave me,' she muttered at him.

'Come into the kitchen and I will tell you everything as we have a cup of tea, Mom.'

Jason took his mother's hand and led her to the kitchen and sat her down at the kitchen table.

'When did you apply for a job,' she asked? 'And what's this crazy crap about you going to California?'

Jason laughed as he started boiling the water for their tea.

'Slow down I will tell you everything Mom. But I do not want you getting yourself worked up into a frenzy. I sent a few samples of a computer program I designed while I was still in high school to a company called Form-a-cell. Which is one of the biggest software companies in the world? It's based out in California. Now they have asked me to come to California to work for them. They have offered me a salary of two hundred thousand a year to start with. That alone is more money than I could make in ten years around here. Therefore, I am going to California with or without your blessing.'

Amanda protested till Jason raised his hand to her. 'I will drive out there because of my fear of flying after what happened to Dad. The plane he was on crashed with no warning signs. And besides, it is only eighteen hundred miles, I can drive that in two-and-a-half days. Well, I must get busy packing, Mom I have lots to do.'

'I dislike it Jason,' Amanda blurted out through her crying. 'You need to stay here close to home you are way too young to be going off so far away on your own.'

'But Mom this is the opportunity of a lifetime for me. And I am going case closed.' Jason's voice rose in his anger at his mother. 'Why am I not allowed to have happiness? You are always sheltering me from life. I am not a child any more I am a grown adult. Why can't you see that now?'

Amanda slid her chair out and stood over him, looming over him. 'You may be eighteen now, but I am still your mother. I will be your mother forever,' she screamed at him in her rage. 'You will regret leaving here this way. You mark my words, son, you will regret your decision to leave here Jason.'

With tears streaming down her face, Amanda Goodson left the kitchen and stomped her way up the stairs to her bedroom. 'Awe man, you see now why I did not want to tell her about the job. I knew she would blow up like this.'

'Well, it looks as if I am being given the silent treatment again. This is not the first time someone forced him to endure the silent treatment. Damn this is not what I needed right now. Your silent treatment will not work on me this time. I am still going to California. I may never get this kind of opportunity again.' Jason screamed these words out into the silent kitchen.

After going upstairs to his bedroom, Jason packed his bags to leave the next morning. Twice he had gone to his mother's door and knocked lightly. 'Mom, are you coming out to talk about this? You need to quit giving me the silent treatment. I really would like to spend the rest of my time here at the house with you. You need to come and talk to me about this please.' he begged his mother.

After several minutes with no response, Jason hung his head down in sadness. 'Fine, I give up he said have it your way. That's the only way in this! Right, it has to be your way.'

Jason headed back to his room, his heart was breaking, but he had to do this for him. He needed a life of his own. So, he finished packing his things again. After some time, Jason collapsed on the bed in exhaustion from the fight with his mother. The last thought he had before drifting off to sleep was how hard his mother had taken the death of his father.

Jason loaded his Range Rover around 8:00 am the next morning, he packed his things in the range rover in silence.

His mother had chosen to not show herself this morning after the fight in the kitchen last night. After loading his car, he still had not heard or seen hide or hair of his mother. This was no surprise to Jason. After walking back up to his mother's room, he knocked on the door several times with no response at all.

He reached out and tried the door handle, locked tight. It would be, he thought.

'Mom, are you in there? Well, I am leaving now. I will see you in a month or maybe two. I should have a nice place to stay by then maybe you can come and visit me out there.'

But there was only silence returned to him. After standing there with tears trickling down his cheeks, 'Well, I love you, Mom, goodbye.

Jason left the house, saying nothing else to his mother. He got into the car and started the motor. Now she will come running out for sure, he thought. After sitting there for five minutes, he saw no sign of his mother. She had not even looked out the window at him. He was watching to see if she looked out, so he could wave goodbye to her. But there was no sign of her. Jason said a brief prayer for luck and safety before he put the car in gear. He pulled away from the curb, leaving his mother to her own thoughts.

Jason turned the car off his street. All the thoughts that were flooding into his mind were thoughts of his mother. She will regret her decision to not say goodbye before leaving. 'She will regret it I can promise you,' he said all this out loud as he turned the corner and headed west towards California.

Jason left Tennessee heading for California with his

mind heavy with the thoughts of how his mother had been acting after the news of him leaving. It had to be this way. There was no other choice with his mother.

Amanda Goodson's way of dealing with hard decisions in life is to hide away in her room, giving people the silent treatment. The only difference this time is I will be eighteen hundred miles away. Out of sight, out of mind, he thought. Although he tried hard to quit thinking of his mother. He had no luck at all, she kept rushing back to the forefront of his mind.

Jason's mother took the death of her husband very hard. Even though Sam Goodson was a travelling salesperson, and his job had kept him on the road most of the time while Jason was growing up. Jason did not know his father all that well. He only got to see for two days every other week. His job kept him on the road for two weeks at a time. Jason was eight years old at the time of his father's death. After the funeral was over, his mother took a five-day hiatus. Leaving Jason to fend for himself. Those five days were hard on Jason. All he had to eat for those days were pop tarts and frozen hot pockets. He did not understand where his mother was or if she was coming back or not. Then on the fifth day she came home and was a different person all together. Amanda Goodson never spoke of her disappearance to Jason she pretended nothing happened at all.

As the miles rolled along Jason tried to occupy his mind with something other than the thoughts of his mother. He wrote all the different state licenses plates he saw on a scrap of paper hoping to see all fifty states. That seemed to help a lot. Although he could not shake the strong feeling he would never see his mother again, and that bothered him terribly.

After getting bored looking at the tags, he kept fumbling with the radio channels. He thought he was losing the station every fifty miles. Jason had been driving all day; he had only stopped twice to fill up his gas tank. Once he stopped at a Wendy's for a burger to go. Tennessee and his mother further and further behind him.

Jason saw a lot of neat things as he drove. Some sights he saw had reminded him of the sights that his father had told him about, in the stories of his travels. Once again, the thoughts of Jason's mother came sneaking back into his mind. This time it was the thought of why his mother had not yet called to check on him. That was highly unlike his mother.

Amanda Goodson was very persistent on the matter of making sure he was all right when he was not at home. With all these thoughts of his mother. Jason never once considered the idea that he would be all the way out in California, all alone and on his own. Jason had slept nowhere without his mother being there. They have always been together. Now it was strange that these thoughts had never entered his mind until now. He suddenly pounded his fist on the steering wheel. Damn I need to quit thinking about my mother. We are both grown adults. Then he said under his breath only she is the one acting like the child. Damn she is driving me crazy even though she is not here with me.

The day and the miles had slipped away; it was now approaching 10 p.m. Jason looked for a motel to pull over for the night. He had not gone thirty miles before deciding to stop for the night. When he spotted the Motel Six. And you all know they will leave a light on for you. This thought brought a smile across his face as he pulled into the parking lot of the Motel Six.

When he entered the motel lobby, his nerves were a jumping jitterbug. He had never done this before I don't know if they will even give me a room or not. But he relaxed as the large plump woman stood up before him with a huge, pleasant smile on her face. How can I help you?

After receiving the key to room number six, Jason grabbed his rucksack out of the car and headed for his room. Exhaustion was dragging on his willpower to move.

When he entered the room, it was dimly lit with a small nightlight by the door. Jason gave no notice to the fact they had left a light on for him. He only threw his bag on the bed and headed for the shower. After a long hot shower with all that endless hot water he felt rejuvenated again. Hell, he felt more alive than he had ever before in his life.

As Jason sat down on his bed smiling, the thoughts of his mother came rushing back to the forefront of his mind. They came rushing in, as powerful as the water flowing over Niagara Falls. He grabbed his head with both hands to stop it from spinning. He grabbed his cell phone and dialed his mother's number. If she doesn't answer I will leave a message that way she will at least know I am all right and still alive.

The phone rang four times and then his mother's voice came on the line. You have reached the Goodson residence, please leave a message, thank you. After the deafening loud tone that blared into Jason's ear he began. Hi, Mom, it's Jason I wanted to let you know that I am OK, and I love you I will try to reach you again tomorrow goodbye. Jason's mind was now spinning rapidly this was so strange he never could not reach his mother before. God, I hope she is OK. I hate we had a fight and now I cannot reach her by phone. I really wanted to tell her I was sorry for the fight. With this thought rapidly racing through his tired mind, Jason drifted off into a troubled sleep.

He had awakened twice with the same horrible dreams. Ones he could not remember once he had awakened. At last, he slipped off into sleep once again. This time the dream or nightmare were like movie clips of his life. The first one was of his young childhood. There he was at five, playing in a mudhole in the backyard. Then he was seven and his dog Sam had just gotten hit by a car in front of their house. Then he was eight. He was there, standing over his father's casket as the dirt was being thrown in on its top. He could smell the fresh dirt. Oh God, he could hear the sobbing all around him loud in his little ears. Jason popped up wide awake. The sweat was running down his face intermingling with the tears. Too exhausted to get up out of the bed, he slid to the other side of the bed where it wasn't soaked in sweat. There he slowly drifted back off to sleep.

The next clip of dreams came like a slap across his face. He was sitting at the kitchen table across from his mother. She was staring at him all wide-eyed. It was more like she was staring through him. Mom, what's wrong he asked? Hello earth to Mom, are you OK? There was no response, she just sat there all wide-eyed staring off into space. Jason sat bolt upright in the bed.

Wow, he would have sworn in court he had just been sitting at the kitchen table with his mother. The smell of the fresh flowers his mother always kept on the kitchen table still lingered in his nose. Wow, what a dream he said out loud to the empty room. This time he did not have a choice he had to get up and go urinate. On the way back from the bathroom, he grabbed his phone and dialed his mother's number regardless of the time of the night.

The phone rang the same four times and his mother's voice came on the line. 'Hello, you have reached the Goodson residence, please leave a message after the beep, thank you.'

There was that deafening, loud tone again. 'Hi mom it's Jason again. Where are you? Why won't you answer the phone?' Anger now setting in, 'If you think for one minute that I will give up and turn around and come home just because you won't answer the phone. I am here to tell you that you would be dead wrong. Anyway, I love you.'

After flipping his phone shut, he tossed it back on the nightstand. He sat back down on the edge of the bed. He was swaying back and forth. His mind swam with crazy thoughts of his mother. I cannot believe she is being this contrary. He looked over at the bedside clock. Only to see that it read 4:00 a.m. Yawning, he flopped back on the bed. His feet were still on the floor when he awoke an hour later.

As he sat up, his entire body throbbed. He started for the shower, trying to remember the nightmares he had suffered through with no luck. OK, I guess I had them because I was so tired from driving all day. Along with worrying about my mother. That had to be it, he said aloud to the steamy empty bathroom.

After a long hot shower, Jason changed clothes and grabbed his bag. He was eager to get back on the road heading west. When he arrived in the office, he observed that they served breakfast. This is great, he thought, I eat before hitting the road. After he turned his key in to the large plump lady with the big smile, he sat down and ate two bowls of cornflakes drenched in chocolate milk.

As he ate his cereal Jason studied his road map. He was keen to get back on the road, even though he got no sleep last night. Jason finished eating, thanked the large plump lady with the big smile and headed out to the Range Rover. Smiling as he walked, he felt a lot better now that his belly was full. He started the Range Rover, pulled out of the parking lot and took a right back onto the freeway. With a big smile on his face, he headed west toward California.

There were a lot of open roads ahead of him and the miles and the day seemed to fly by in the blink of an eye. At one point he thought he needed gas. But when he checked the gauges, the gas gauge read full. Startled at this new discovery. When did I stop for gas? He was getting very shaken up by this. I know I must have stopped for gas; the tank is full. But how did I do it without remembering it? So, he then saw a sign for a rest area. After he pulled into the rest area he got out of the car and walked around. He was muttering to himself.

'How far have I driven without realizing it? Shit,' he said aloud, 'I could've run off the road and killed myself for Christ's sake.' He then slapped the side of his face hard. It made a loud smack in the still afternoon air. Jason was pacing back and forth beside the Range Rover. 'You must get a hold of yourself,' he said. Taking a deep breath and letting it out slowly. Only then did he begin to calm down.

At this point he headed into the restroom to relieve himself. As he opened the bathroom door, the thoughts of his mother rammed their way back into his mind. I will have to call before I take off again. He slipped quietly in the bathroom.

After urinating and washing his hands and face, Jason felt refreshed and alive again. On the way back to the Range Rover he made a detour to the vending machine to grab a coke and a snack. As the coke machine was dispensing the soda the sound coming from the machine sounded like voices. Then his coke plopped into the tray below. Wow, he thought, that sounded like voices. He could not help it, his curiosity got the best of him. He shoved three more quarters into the machine. This time he heard it with clarity. It was his mother's voice. You will regret your decision to leave me. Jason held on to the coke he had in his hand and ran for his car.

Once he was on the freeway again Jason's hands had a death grip on the steering wheel. His entire body was trembling with fear. He had been heading into the setting sun for three hours now. He could not shake the feeling that something was wrong with his mother. He could feel it in his bones.

When he had topped the next rise in the road it surprised him to see a super large billboard spanning across both lanes of the road. The billboard was written in large block letters: last chance, last gas for two hundred miles, get it now.

Jason pulled to the shoulder of the road and marveled at the large sign. Wow, I guess I have made it to the desert. No life for two hundred miles. He sat and stared in awe for a short time.

He pulled back out into the road and drove the quarter of a mile to the last gas station for two hundred miles.

Jason pulled up close to the gas pumps and got out. He stretched, bowing his back in unique positions. Then he looked up into the bright, clear twilight sky. Wow, what a beautiful day this has been. He walked around to the gas pumps. Jason looked around as he walked, but the place looked deserted. He smiled, deserted at the edge of the desert. He inserted his debit card into the card reader. He took the gas nozzle and inserted it into the gas tank inlet. As Jason was locking the lever in place, the thought of his mother's face came rushing back. Damn, I must call her this may be my last place for a phone signal. He latched the lever down. Went to the passenger window and reached in and grabbed his phone from the passenger seat.

Jason Goodson leaned his hips against the side of the Range Rover. He dialed his mother's phone number once again. On the first ring, a static spark from the cell phone ignited the gas fumes, causing Jason Goodson's entire world to explode in a massive fireball from hell. Totally leveling over a half of a mile area around the gas station.

AT that same moment in the small cottage of Amanda Goodson, the phone rang only once.

Unbeknownst to Amanda Goodson, that one ring fell upon deaf ears. If you were there, you would see Amanda Goodson sprawled across her bed. Both of her wrists would be slashed to the bone. The blood pools around her body have already turned crusty and dried; she had slashed her wrists after she had left the kitchen that night.

The End

TOTAL ABYSS

Randy Scofield is a forty-eight-year-old electrician. He has worked hard his whole life. For many years he lived from pay check to pay check. No matter how hard he tried, he could not get ahead in life. Oh, but his dreams are bigger than life. The real harshness of life is that most people never accomplish their dreams they let them die out.

Randy was working on a boat dock one day. They were on a lake way up in the western mountains. The sun was glowing; the air had a slight breeze to it. This lake was sparsely populated in the area he was working, so it was silent and serene. There was only a handful of houses around and not one of them was near the water's edge. They were all nestled in the high sloping mountainside.

The day, bright and humid, a typical June morning. Randy and Jim Miller, his helper, spent the first hour pulling the wires they needed into the flexible pipe they will pull out to the main dock platform. Even though it is early, Randy was now hot and sticky with sweat.

'Yes, Jim, I am looking forward to getting in the water today it's muggy as hell out here.'

'That's for sure,' Jim replied. Now that the wires are pulled into the pipe, the trick is to get the pipe fed over top of everything underneath the bottom of the walkway leading to the boat dock.

Randy slipped off the bank into the knee-deep water at

the edge of the lake.

He gasped, 'Oh shit.'

Jim laughed, 'Is it cold you wussy?'

'Hell, no, it is not cold at all. In fact, it is as hot as bath water. This is not refreshing at all,' Randy remarked.

Randy takes the end of the pipe and makes his way under the walkway leading to the dock. This walkway is the longest one they have ever worked on. The walkway itself is over a hundred feet long before you get to the dock part.

He started feeding the pipe over the top of the braces holding up the walkway. It did not take Randy long before the water was up to his waist. Randy had pulled the pipe out about a thirty-foot section from the shoreline when the floor of the lake sloped downward at a fast pace.

'OK,' he called to Jim, 'the dock has gotten too high for me to reach I will need the ladder.'

Moments later, a six-foot ladder descended the side of the walkway. Taking the ladder with great dread, Randy placed it under the walkway. Ladders inside the lake was never a good idea. Randy knows first-hand what it feels like being thrown off a ladder into the lake. He still has the scars to prove it.

The placement of the ladder in the lake is tricky, you never know where the soft spots are till you get the ladder set up. When you step on it, you will see which leg sinks the most and adjust your weight to stay off that ladder leg as much as you can.

The ladder will have to be moved around twice between each set of pylons. By now the water had reached a height of four feet. That's not good for someone who is only five foot eight inches tall. At this point Randy must shuffle his feet along the bottom with caution. It is tricky to make your way around a set of pylons. You never know when the bottom has been dredged out. He did not want his head submerged without a warning. After the ladder legs cleared the pylon, Randy loosened his grip on the ladder only a little, so that the ladder would slide through his hands. And slip into place on the backside of the pylon. When the ladder started down, Randy stepped up on the first rung, so he could ride the ladder down into place. He knew that by standing on the first step the back legs would hit the bottom first and he could guide the front legs down as they descended. The front legs seemed to descend at a slower rate than the back legs.

To Randy's surprise the front legs of the ladder never touched the bottom. Suddenly he was being sucked downward. Randy had just enough time to close his mouth and take in a deep breath with his nose. Then he was underwater, descending downward through the waters. He still had his grip on the ladder, but he was falling faster now.

Randy's eyes stung inside their sockets. Now he was deep enough that the pressure on his body wanted to force the last breath he had taken from his lungs. With great effort he battled through, keeping his last breath in. In less time than it takes to take a deep breath, Randy saw the brown murky water change color before his eyes. The next thing he knew, everything went black. Something slammed his body with a rush of bitter cold water. It chilled him to the bone. It was trying to make him gasp, but he held on to his last breath.

In the blink of an eye, Randy saw tiny white specks of light inside the darkness. He was now free-falling through the blackness. His mind now concentrated on holding the last breath he took just before going under. With his mind preoccupied he did not understand when he had let go of the ladder.

Free-falling into an abyss of darkness, Randy's face had turned a slight shade of blue. He was starved of oxygen. He really panicked when the white specks rushed toward him at the speed of light. Randy has been holding his breath for four minutes now. He is slowly reaching his breaking point. He knew in his heart he could not hold his breath for much longer now.

Randy has reached that critical point, he could no longer hold on to his last breath. Randy closed his eyes and prepared to release his final breath. Suddenly he landed on a cushion of air. It forced his precious last breath from his lungs in a loud whoosh sound.

Opening his eyes, Randy saw he was not on a cushion at all. He was inside a bubble. The inside of the bubble felt like someone made it out of a memory foam mattress. But it was all clear, he could see through it like a picture window.

Panic now setting in as Randy clambered all around the sphere someone trapped him in to no avail.

After a few minutes he sat back gasping for breath. Wanting deep breaths but all he could manage was short shallow breaths. As smart as Randy was, he took slow tiny breaths. As his breathing slowed his eyes became clearer. He was now seeing a vast sea of round spheres. Millions of them shimmering in a faint purple glow.

Randy gasped while he scrambled backwards. In the sphere right next to him was a lady her face was twisted as if she was in agony. Her eyes bulged from her skull. Her eyes look as if they would burst at any moment.

Oh God, he thought, is that how I will die. When he had gotten a hold of himself, he looked at her again more closely. He noticed that she was wearing eighteenth century clothing. Holy shit, he thought, how long she has been in that thing.

The thoughts of the dress she was wearing raced across his mind like a bolt of lightning. What replaced it was complete and utter awe. The spheres were moving. Bumping into one another and then floating off in a new direction. Some spheres just popped up on top of others. Only to settle back down into the next available gap. In this vast sea of bubbles.

It was a breath-taking sight. Stunned in silence, Randy's sphere collided with another. Scrambling around to see what was in this one. The sight inside the next sphere knocked him off his feet. He was now face to face with the notorious Jimmy Hoffa. Someone dressed him just as all the articles had described him. So, this is where you have been hanging out all this time, Randy spoke out loud, here at the bottom of Lake Hickory. Holy shit, where the hell am I.

Using his legs along with his back against the side, Randy stood up, he wanted a better view. He looked out over the vast sea of spheres in amazement. He thought of the Beatle's 'Lucy in the Sky with Diamonds'. All the spheres sparkled in the faint purple glow. As far as you could see in any direction were spheres. They were in all sizes.

Some had planes and ship, some of them had people. There were animals and many other things as well. Some of them even looked from other worlds. One of the amazing things where they all looked new. Everything looked as if it was preserved and was being showcased in a museum.

All of a sudden, his sphere was bumped again, looking around Randy saw the blue six-foot ladder he was using before he ended up here.

Sliding back down to the floor of his sphere, the realization hit him like a ton of bricks. Randy let out a long heavy sigh, I am dead. He spoke this out loud. He then thought of his family, they would be out at the lake searching for him. But they would never find his body. He is floating in a bubble field. With this thought, he wept uncontrollably.

The weeping slowed to small shudders. Can this be heaven he thought? Why would inanimate objects be in heaven? Randy slowly took little shallow breaths, he laid on his back and looked up into the purple sky. He could barely make out a faint swirling motion in the sky.

The movement he saw in the sky was soothing to him. He noticed it was becoming harder to take a breath. If he had thought about the idea he would run out of air, he would have tried harder to conserve it.

Randy Soufflé's last fading thought was, I have fallen into the Bermuda Triangle. He struggled to take his last breath. His mind now ticking to a stop he thought. It's the triangle, it moves from place to place taking what it wants when it wants. Randy's eyelids slowly eased shut there was one more shallow breath, and everything went dark. And Randy's sphere continued its endless bobbing into eternity. Forever changing places with the other spheres.

THE END

EVIL

Evil is described, talked about, and feared. 'Someone who may be told they are evil may also be wicked, mean and ruthless. Some people also believe something relates evil to demons and Satan himself. If you will allow me, I will tell you of a tale whispered and rumored about for a hundred years here in these parts. You look like a fine young man. So, I will try to help with your article there. Let me see here, I believe it all started in the spring of nineteen twenty-six. Some of what I will tell you I saw with my own eyes. I did! I have seen some of these things and they cannot be unseen. Then there are parts of the story rumored about in and around town. But the stories did not go too far from these parts of the country, maybe two counties. We like to keep things to ourselves in these parts you know.

'Well, let me see, it was a hot muggy morning in late May. I remember just how hot and sticky the air was. It had been so hot and dry that month you could see the salt forming on your arms when you sweated. I was ten years old that year my mother and I were sitting on this same porch when hell's child came into this world. Right over yonder across the way there.'

He pointed to the large farmhouse across the road.

'It was around eight a.m. we had just finished breakfast and came out to enjoy what was the coolest part of the day. Then it began as a slight breeze. My mother smiled as she turned her head to face the oncoming breeze.

'I tell you Sam, is it OK if I call you Sam?'

'Yes, sir you can.'

'OK, I tell you Sam, that breeze felt sweeter than life itself. Then all at once the breeze picked up the loose dust from the dry ground and it soon forced us to retreat inside the house. Soon you could not see the old doc's place over yonder. Then the wind became a gale, you could see nothing outside for the dust. The house was shaking, so I feared it would come down on top of us. It felt as if the whole house was swaying in the breezes.

'It stopped just as abruptly as it had started. The air went right back to being hot and sticky but it had a faint foul stale odor to it, you could only faintly smell it occasionally. But there were some folks never smelled it but a lot of folks, me included, could smell it. It was a rotten smell way beyond the decayed smell of a rotten animal. This smell was the smell of death himself. In my ninety years I have encountered nothing that stank like the air after the dust storm of twenty-six. Shortly after the storm was over, that young lady, Miss Cowen was her name, she came over to fetch my mother saying the doctor needed her help. As my mother got up to leave, I also stood up I wanted to go see what was going on over there too. That's when Miss Cowen spoke up, "No sir, young man you must stay here." My mother spoke up, "I will be right back Tommy." And they walked away.

'So, I sat back down to wait on my mother to get back. That's when I heard the blood-curdling screams. I was ten at the time you know. But I jumped up from the chair I was sitting in and went to my room. I lay with my head under the pillow and I could still hear them screams. Piercing my brain, I have no idea how the three of them could stand to be that close to the screams, the screaming seemed to last for hours before they stopped all together.

'I tell you, Sam, it scared me. I had heard nothing like that before in my life. I later found out it was the screams of death. It was dark when my parents came home. My mother washed her hands for half an hour scrubbing them raw I noticed. She turned and smiled at me, her eyes were puffy and bloodshot. "Tommy be a dear and grab the sandwich meat from the icebox. I am dogged tired, so we will have a sandwich for dinner."

"Sure, Mom," and I preceded to grab the stuff she requested.

The three of us sat down and ate in silence. After dinner, my father asked me to go to bed so he could have a talk with my mother. I agreed and kissed my mother's cheek and left the room. I made my way up the stairs, my mind running a mile a minute. There had to be a way I could listen in to their conversation. That's when I headed for my room, I slipped out my window to hide at the corner of the house. I could hear everything they said, and not be spotted by my parents.

Sam, this is what I heard my mother tell my father that night after the great dust storm. 'In the storm's heart this old lady of about sixty shows up at the doctor's door, he barely heard her pounding on his door. As he opened the door she fell inside at his feet. He could see she was in labor. He yelled for Sarah to come and help him. They could only get her inside the door and that's when Sarah came and got me.'

My mother said, "When I arrived, we got her to a bed

she was lifeless I thought she was dead. I really did Bob! She was cold and slimy to the touch. The feel reminded me of how a slug would feel. Gross, I tell you. Then with a hard jerk she had another contraction. The doctor gasped, oh my God it's coming out I can see the head. The old lady's eyes popped open, all I could see of them was the whites there were no pupils or iris just white,' she told my father. All I could do is sit there with my mouth gaped open listening in silence at what my mother was saying.

My father asked, "What in the hell is a sixty-year-old blind woman doing having a child at her age?"

'I do not understand why, but it was creepy all the same. But wait, it gets a lot worse. "Once the head emerged, Doc Brown grasped it in his large hands and yelled for me to help her push. Which meant for me to push on her stomach to help the baby's shoulders to come free. So, I positioned my hands on her stomach. I told her to push one more time and it would be over. Then I pushed slightly on her stomach as the doctor pulled. Suddenly the old lady screamed. Bob, it was not a normal scream, it was otherworldly. And it was so ear-splitting I knew it would burst my eardrums. That's when the doctor stumbled backwards screaming himself, 'Oh God, oh God no not this no,' and he went to his knees holding the child in his out-stretched arms."

My father sat in silence as he looked at her in horror. "I rushed over to him," she began, "and nearly puked right then." She suddenly shuddered and dry heaved only once before she continued. "There was Doc Brown on his knees. The baby in his hands. Bob, it had two handfuls of his mother's intestines in its tiny hands. Oh God, Bob, he was chewing on them. Chewing them as if he was in a rage."

My father said nothing, he got up and strolled to the end of the porch and puked up his dinner. "I am so sorry Bob are you OK?"

Wiping his mouth, "Yes; I am OK. Wow, that's got to be a horror story for sure. I glad Tommy is not out here to hear this."

Oh, but I was, and it stunned me frozen like a statue. My father sat back down, "I am guessing the old lady died!"

"Yes, she bled out. I took the baby, released his mother's guts from his hands and took him over to the changing table and placed him face down. I did not want to look into his eyes at all. Sarah was in shock. Sarah go get Mrs Gillen. When she did not respond I slapped her in the face hard. That got her moving, go get Mrs Gillen."

"'With some effort I got Doc Brown back on his feet. "Did you see that!" he asked?

"Yes, now we must get things in order, Mrs Gillen will be here soon. I sent Sarah after her."

"Why do we need her," he asked?

"Because she had just had a baby two weeks prior. This baby would need to nurse. The mother is not able to do it." And they turned to look at the old lady with her white eyes staring up blankly at the ceiling. I had to slap myself and the loud sound in in the quiet room got us going.

'The doctor took care of cleaning up the baby. I cleaned up all the blood. I also covered the old lady; I could not take looking at those eyes. Doc Brown closed them twice but they sprang open both times. Sarah returned saying, "Mrs Gillen would be right here."

"OK," I said, "don't let her come back here. Keep her in the front parlor. I will talk with her up there."

"OK," Sarah said with a frown. and she left the room. Thirty minutes later Sarah came back and said, "Mrs. Gillen is here."

"OK, thanks Sarah, here, you finish mopping I will go talk to her alone I will be right back."

'Entering the parlor, "Hi Nancy, how are you?"

"I am good, Brenda, Sarah said you needed to speak with me urgently. What's wrong, you look as if you have seen the devil himself?"

'Well, I told her what had happened. Leaving out the guts everywhere part of the story. When I had finished, she said "Oh, my God, that's so awful. But what can I do?"

Brenda smiled. "Well, I was hoping you would let him nurse for a day or two? Just till we can find a suitable home for him."

"Don't see why not, that little infant can't eat that much? Sure, Brenda I will do that?" Nancy said, smiling. "You're an angel, Nancy. I will be right back with the baby."

'Brenda entered the exam room. Once there they pounced on her, both Sarah and Doc Brown. "Well, what did she say? Will she do it?"

Brenda held up her hand, "OK, wait, one at a time, please. Yes, she will nurse him for the two days till we find someone to take him."

The Doc sighed, "Thank God."

'Brenda took the child back to the parlor. There she handed the child to Nancy. "Ahh, how cute he is," Nancy pulls up her shirt to reveal her plump breast. She places the child down next to her nipple he took right to it. Nancy looked up, "Wow he sure does have a tight grip on the nipple."

Smiling, Brenda said, "I am glad he gets to nurse."

"Yes, they need the nourishment the first few days,"

Nancy began but then her face turned up in a frown. That's when she screamed. She jumped to her feet, letting the child hit the floor with a loud thud. I gasped. "What are you doing?" I yelled as I fell to my knees beside the child. Taking him in my arms I turned to face the screaming woman. But what I saw stopped me cold. Nancy was screaming, holding her breast. I could see blood dripping through her fingers. "Nancy, move your hand let me see." That's when Sarah and the doc came running into the parlor. She lifted her hand from her breast. Blood and milk insanely gushed from the massive hole in her breast. The nipple completely gone now. Revealing a two-inch crater in the center of her breast. One look and Nancy fainted, hitting the floor hard with her face.

'Everyone was screaming, myself including. I reached down and picked the child up reluctantly. He was also screaming. his face was smeared with blood. It grinned at me, Bob, and for only a second; I saw a mouth full of needle-sharp teeth. Then they disappeared. But I know I what I saw Bob, don't look at me as if I were crazy. I know what I saw, the new-born had teeth that disappeared. When I picked it up, I swear it weighed more now, a lot more than when he was born. It was as if it grew ten pounds on that one bite.

That's when my father spoke for the first time in a good while. "Wait, you said that when it was born you saw it tearing at his mother's guts therefore it must have had teeth. It is very difficult to tear open the intestines. I know that from skinning animals."

'I tell you sonny I know for sure it scared my parents, but I was also frightened, I wet myself right there in the bushes. In my mind I was picturing one of those piranha fish I had seen in the *National Geographic* magazines with all of them there teeth you know.

'Anyways, my mother took the baby back to the crib being careful to keep the thing she carried at arm's length from her breast. I then placed the thing into the crib with a blanket. When I returned to the parlor, Bob, the doctor was covering Nancy with a towel. I gasped oh no, and the doctor turned towards me with tears streaming down his face. His eyes were almost swollen shut. All he said was! She bled out. Just that quick she bled out. Poor Sarah was laying against the wall in the fetal position, whimpering softly. "Oh, Bob, at that point I had to leave, I could not breath, it was as if an invisible hand were squeezing my throat, I needed fresh air now.

'"I went out to the back porch and sobbed. I was the one that asked Nancy over to help and now she is dead too." She now wept as my father put his hands on her shoulder and pulled her close to him. I had tears running myself sonny. As if that was not tragic enough.

'She sighed, straightened up and began again. After thirty minutes I went back in to check on everything. My first stop was the baby. The thing. Anyhow, he was not there. The crib was empty, baby blanket and all. I rushed back to the parlor to see what else had happened. As I arrived in the parlor, I found the doctor mopping the floor. Sarah was still in the fetal position whimpering, only now she was on the sofa. "Where's the baby I gasped? He is not in the crib."

Doc Brown just looked at me as if I was insane. "He is in the crib, I saw him a few minutes ago when I went for the mop."

"Well, he is not there now." I looked down and saw tiny footprints in the blood. I nearly fainted just then. Bob, how could an infant just get up and walk out. Hell, he was only four hours old. Then again, there they were, footprints plain as day headed out the door.

'The two of us rushed out to the porch. There was nothing but blowing sand. It was as if it had just vanished into thin air. We just stood there looking at each other in silence for the longest time. Doc Brown broke the silence. "Go get the constable, tell him to just come and see me to find out the details. Do not let him know there is a bloody mess up here." He sighed I guess you will need to stop by the mill and let Will Truman know about his wife. "He will not take it well that's my guess."

'So, after I went downtown to fetch the constable and Mr Truman, I came back to help clean up the blood. Well, I tell you this, Bob, he was right! Will Truman did not take it well, in fact he took it fatally. Nancy was still on the floor with a sheet over when Will arrived. I told him I was sorry about what happened, and he ignored me completely. He fell to his knees screaming, "No, oh God no," that is when he grabbed the sheet and ripped it back revealing the gross corpse of his dead wife. He shrieked and before I could get across the room to him, he snatched up a pair of scissors and jammed them into his heart, he collapsed dead over top of his wife. That was all I could take for one day. I fainted then. Now we have a dead old lady with her intestines torn out, we have a dead lady with her breast ripped open, now her husband dead of a self-inflicted stab wound, two children without parents. One of whom is missing. What a hell of a day this has turned out to be.

'When I came to, the doctor, and the constable were kneeling beside me, each with a hand rubbing it vigorously. "You OK?" the doc asked.

"Yes, I think so, is he dead?"

"Yes, he is," the constable said in a whisper.

'My father spoke for the first time in a long while. "I can't believe three people have died today alone."

"Yes, I know they sent out a search party for the baby, but they never found him. There was not any kind of sign of the baby."

'Bob, my mother cried, and I watched as my father tried to console her, but she just kept right on crying. That was my cue to go back to my room. First, I had to stop at the washroom to dry the tears off my face. I know I would have nightmares about all that I had heard.

'Come to find out I had no nightmares at all. Would you like something to drink Sam?'

'Why yes, I would thank you.'

'Well, you run to the icebox and grab us both a pop or a beer whichever you prefer. I am parched from all this gabbing.' After they both took long deep swigs of their beer I continued.

'It was three days later that I saw the thing that wreaked all the havoc at Doc Brown's house. I was on my way through the woods to the creek to do a little fishing. The morning sun shone brightly that morning. I remember thinking wow what a glorious day it is. There were little patches of light shining through the open spaces in the forest. It was in one of these little patches of light I saw it. I stopped as if I had hit a brick wall. Stunned, I stared in utter horror at what I saw before me. It looked like a boy, it was maybe two-foot-tall, butt naked and dirty as the ground itself.

'The image of what I saw will be forever burned into my mind, Sam. The thing was standing on two legs just like I was, but he had a small cat in his hands and his mouth was tearing into the cat's underbelly with the fierceness of a piranha fish. I stood with my mouth gaped open 'til I saw one of the cat's intestines burst and splatter a cream-colored goo across the thing's face. I gagged just then, so I dropped my fishing pole and ran. I ran like the wind; I was too scared to look back to see if I was being followed or not. At some point I lost control of my stomach and I puked as I ran. It flew all down the front of my shirt, I kept running.

'I ran straight to the constable's office hoping he was there and not gone out on an investigation or something. But when I burst through the door panting out of breath, he jumped from his seat with his right hand already unstrapping the clasp of his revolver, all in the blink of an eye. "Boy, what the hell is wrong with you bursting in here like a mad dog I could have shot you?"

Gasping for breath, with my hands on my knees, I choked out what I saw in the woods. Each word came out after a huge deep breath. "I saw the thing that killed those people at Doc Brown's place I saw in the forest just now. I was on my way to the creek to go fishing and I saw it in the woods." Tears were now streaming down my face as I tried to breathe and talk at the same time. "It was eating a cat raw," I screamed.

This statement got his fat ass moving. "It was eating a cat?" he asked

"Yes," I said in a low whisper as if I did not want the thing to hear me snitch on it. "He was! It was ripping the guts out of it when I saw him, so I dropped my fishing pole and ran straight here to tell you what I saw." It scared me that day, but I knew in my heart I did the right thing by fetching the constable.

'"Can you show me where you saw it?" My breathing had slowed now, and I nodded my head yes.

'When we got to the street, there were five other men standing there. "Is everything all right, Walt?" One man asked.

"Yes, young Tommy here saw the thing that attacked at the doc's house in the woods. You guys want to help me search the area for it?"

"Sure," they all chimed in together. And off we went towards the woods.

'I will tell you this, Sam had I known what was going to happen that day I would have stayed home. Once we got into the edge of the forest, the constable said in a low voice, "Spread out only fifteen paces apart that way maybe we can surround him easy." They spread out as ordered. I stayed right next to the constable. We were soon at the spot where I had dropped my fishing pole. There I pointed toward a small clearing. Something covered the clearing and surrounding trees in blood. It looked like a massacre had occurred. Which I guess it did. The creature was gone, all that remained was the skin and the bones of the cat. It had devoured all the meat and guts. At this point all the others had gathered around to see the carnage left behind. Two of the men ran to the nearest tree and puked. Another man just kept repeating oh Jesus over and over.

'OK fellers, spread out and let's find this damn thing. Whatever the hell it is."

One man shouted, "It is a demon sent from Hell. For it to do the things it's done in this town."

"That's for sure," someone else spoke up.

"No matter now, let's find it, OK. All right now, kid, we will take it from here you head home now."

"No way, sir, I am here now I will stay and help find this thing."

I was so scared that I was shaking. Everyone fanned out looking for this terrible creature. After only ten steps from the clearing now and off to my left came a shriek of agony. "What the hell?" the constable yelled, and everyone converged on the sound. There was Bill Hastily laying on the ground screaming, "It got my leg". His right leg was gone just below the knee. There was blood gushing from the ragged wound. I threw up all over the back of the constable's leg. I just could not hold it any longer.

Bill Hastily screamed, "FUCK," and his body went limp. His eyes just rolled over to expose just pure white. A murmur of "Oh shit," began.

"What now, Earl?"

"What the fuck are we dealing with here?"

"Christ, I don't know, you guys know just as much as I do."

'Sam,' I said shaking my head, 'fear is something you only think you know. I can honestly say there are perhaps only a handful of people that can say they have faced the Devil, and lived to tell about it.'

Sam gasped and I could see little round balls of sweat standing out on his forehead. 'You OK son?' I asked?

'Yes, sir,' he said with quivering lips. 'Just excited, please continue.'

I smiled, 'OK, if you insist. Well, we were standing there all in a semi-circle. Looking everywhere, frantically, there was no sign of the thing anywhere. That's when John Hurcheons uttered a single yelp. As we turned, I screamed, the thing was on top of John's chest, chewing at his throat. The constable grabbed his gun and fired, the sound was deafening, my ears rang like church bells. The first shot tore off the front of John's forehead, his brains exploding outward in gooey chunks. The thing whirled its head toward us now. I do not want to lie to you, Sam, I pissed myself, sure as shit stinks. I saw it leap toward us. Our eyes locked together and I heard the creature screaming inside my head. I could not understand it and in an instant its head exploded. I fell to the ground sobbing. Sure, I would be the one eaten next. Then I felt a hand on my shoulder, "It's OK, son it's dead. I looked up and scrambled backwards uttering a small cry as I did this.

'Right there next to me, eyeball to eyeball, was the Devil himself Sam. Scout's honor it was a male child. It had all the male works you know, cock and balls, but the head had small horns protruding from his skull right above the eyebrows. It had a mouth full of razor-looking teeth. The eyes they were as red as hot coals, seeming to burn brighter and brighter till the thing suddenly burst into flames, I had to turn my face the heat was so intense. It felt as if it would burn your eyes out. Then it disappeared leaving only a charred spot on the ground. It's a maybe two-foot square patch. Still to this day nothing grows there in that spot. The foliage is all lush and green around it, but that spot remains bare.

'You can make your way up there and take those photo things if you want to try. But many a folk have tried in the past and they all come out blurred. After I turned eighty, I had quit going up there even though it's always in my head screaming come back Tommy come back Tommy. So now I am too old to make the hike. I don't reckon I will be around these parts much longer. That damn old cancer you know got in my guts. All I have now is waiting to die. That's why you got the dream story of a lifetime, Sam.' With a cough, 'Well, I guess this is the end of my tale, Sam. I hope it will make a good story for you,' and his body went limp, he fell forward face first onto the floor. A tiny trickle of blood traced the wrinkle down his chin as Sam turned him on his back and knelt by his side.

'Shush, don't try to talk.'

'No, I have to clear my conscience,' he coughed. 'Some of this I may have read in a book. but when I looked into the Devil's eyes that day, he told me I would die on this day. I called you to write the story, in fact I did not want to die alone.'

His body expelled his last breath.

The End

THE LOST PLATEAU

My story begins in Perdida Mesa which known in English as lost plateau. Perdida Mesa is a small island just off the coast of southern Mexico. It's about a half a mile from any other land mass. The maps and charts declare it to be uninhabitable. From the sky the island looks like a square except with a round ring of trees for its whole interior area. Perdida Mesa is two hundred yards long and two hundred yards wide. No one knows anything of its origin. One day it was not there the next it was, say the locals.

From all the research done on the island, they say the same thing. I also must add that research includes government documents, maps and charts. There's even a hundred different legends and many rumors about the island. But the only fact found would be that no one has ever stepped foot on the island. I know that you are thinking if the island has a shoreline of rocks how can you not get onto the island. Every document written about the island, of which there are not that many in existence today as most were destroyed, say as you approach the shoreline within a few yards of the island you will pass out and wake back up several yards away from the island. After many tries to get onto the island the Mexican government declared there was some mysterious radiation field causing the affects, therefore, the government condemned the island and declared it to be off limits to everyone, no exceptions.

Unknown to the rest of the world the island was in fact inhabited. Just not on the surface but underneath the island. There, down under ten feet of rocks and soil, was a bunker underground. It was 200 yards by 200 yards. Inside the bunker, there was a small section walled off to act as the living room area. Scattered about the living room were a few pieces of 1970s furniture. In the opposite corner there was a small kitchenette with a table and six chairs. Along one side of the wall there were six small, ten by ten rooms with heavy doors with keypad locks on them. The rest of the bunker was storage and Laboratories along with a small operating room.

In June 2006 after being diagnosed with terminal cancer the doctors gave me six months to live. That's when my doctor referred me to a support group that had just been started up by his brother-in-law. At the time I had no choice but to go to the meeting. I needed someone I could talk too. I have no family. Both my parents are dead. I was an only child, so after the car accident that had killed them both when I was nine, I lost all the family I had. Therefore, I made plans to attend the meeting the next evening. All I know is this was a support group to help anyone dealing with terminal cancer.

That's all my doctor knew about the group was that it started with his brother-in-law. I arrived at Monson convention center at quarter till six. As I walked into room six as directed by the signs, it was a small conference room and I noticed that I was the first one to arrive. I checked my watch six on the nose. Maybe I have come to the wrong room was just crossing my mind when a young woman dressed in a bright red dress with curves to die for entered the room. Along with the red dress she also had ruby red lipstick to match the dress. On a set of the lushest lips I ever saw on a woman. She was also wearing a large white hat set askew on the side of her head with a large red bow tied around it. It made her look stunning. With a heart-warming smile she asked is this the room for the terminal cancer group. My mind was racing with thoughts of how beautiful she was. When the thought, oh yes and I would love to spend my last days with you. As I tried to answer her only a small squeak came out. 'Yes, madam it is, or I think it is anyway we are the only ones here now.'

'Hi, I am Henry Landing!'

'Hi, I am Cindy Help-Land.'

There was a brief monument of awkward silence just before a young man dressed in a suit and a lab coat came strolling in.

'Hello, I am Doctor Swine. I see we are missing one of you. Someone told me there would be three of you.'

Then with a wave of his hand, 'no matter, time is of the essence here, therefore I shall not beat around the bush. I know you are Cindy Help-Land, I also know you have terminal cancer. Your doctor informed you that you only had six months to live and I know that you have no family and you are a loner. I am here to offer you a way to beat the odds if you will allow me.'

She gasped in a deep breath all the while she had the look of horror on her face. Doctor Swine raised his hand to her. I will explain everything in depth in due time. As he turned to look at me, and you sir are Henry Landing, you are in the same shape as Miss Help-Land with cancer and no family. I am offering the both of you a chance to see if we can extend your life here on Earth. I don't know how long but anytime longer than six months would be better than no chance at all. As I have mentioned before, time is of the essence if you agree to this study we will need to leave tonight. I know this is short notice but we're pressed for time so we must go quickly. There will be a long flight, so I can explain more to you on that as we fly but I must assure you, that time is of the essence.

I will need an answer within the next ten minutes. I will also step out of the room and give you time to think it over. He left the room as swiftly as he had come in. That was weird as hell after he had left the room. The two of us standing there looking dumbfounded.

'What is he saying?' I began.

When she blurted out, 'he wants us to be Guinea pigs?'

'Wow, this too much, my head is spinning so fast I can't breathe.'

Reaching out for his shoulder, 'here, sit down,' she said, 'and take shallow breaths.'

She sat down next to me and said, 'Oh my God, what to do. I don't want to die.'

'Yes,' I said with a heavy sigh. 'I don't want to get dead myself. I have nothing to lose, he was right about me not having a family and no real friends either. I will take any chance to beat this thing, I will take that chance.'

'Well, if you put it that way it's understandable, I don't want to die alone, he was right about me as well.'

'How the hell did he know all that stuff about us?'

'I have an idea, but I want to find out how he knows. Yes, I want to know myself, so I will go too.'

'Well, we can find out together at least.'

'Hey that's a big plus already,' as she smiled at me.

As promptly as he said he would, Doctor Swine came back into the room. 'OK I must leave now so are you interested?'

'They both agreed at the same time as if in stereo.

'We agree to go with you.'

'That's fantastic, but I must insist we leave now, we have a plane to catch.'

As we left the small convention center building at a brisk pace, I had a thousand questions jumping into my mind. Once outside we entered a long black limousine. I was unprepared to jump right into the interrogation of the so-called Doctor Swine. Before I could say anything, we had been thrown backwards in our seats as the driver sped off like a bat out of hell. Stunned at how fast all this was happening I burst out with, 'WHAT IN THE BLUE HELL is wrong with you?'

That's when Cindy spoke up. 'Why are we in such a rush? You need to explain yourself and fast.'

'Hell, yea.' I added feeling myself growing very impatient.

'Well now, I will explain everything as we go along. For starters, the need for the rush is crucial to our success. we have a very fine timeline to get to our destination.

'Where is our destination anyway?' Henry demanded. 'You have rushed us off to God knows where. I am feeling kidnapped here.'

'Oh, I can assure you Mr Landing it is nothing of the sort I am only here to help.'

Just then we wheeled into a small airport that looked more like a ghost town than an airport. The light was fading into the sunset as quickly as we were moving. But in the fading light I could just make out a helicopter sitting on the tarmac.

'I asked the good doctor, 'Are we taking a helicopter?'

'Yes, we are going to my private lab. It's on a private small island called Perdida Mesa.'

Cindy gasped in horror, What! Isn't that island off limits to everyone? Besides its uninhabitable, has been forever?'

'Oh, I beg to differ,' the doctor replied with a smile. 'I see you know your geography Miss Help-Land.'

As we lurched to a halt with a screech of tires. the back doors swung open as soon as we had stopped, the blades of an old military helicopter started to rotate. As they led us toward the cargo hold, I saw on the side of the aircraft it was a Sikorsky R-6, a military transport helicopter.

'God, this thing looks like an old and battered heap of metal. I hope we are not going far in this hunk of junk.' The doctor leading the way, we headed through the loading door realizing we knew nothing about him, but we put our lives in his hands. Once inside the aircraft we took our seats on one of the padded benches that lined both walls. There was not much room left in the cargo hold with the huge wooden crate in there with us.

Dr Swine leaned in close and he said, 'There are straps to buckle in with and headphones to dampen the noise. With the high noise level, we cannot have a conversation.'

He was yelling at this point already as the massive blades beat the surrounding air. I then noticed that Cindy was leaning in to hear him also, we nodded our heads and strapped in.

Cindy was on my left; she was expressing total shock and horror on her face. I thought damn she is going into shock. I looked to the doctor on my right as I reached for my headphones; I asked, 'is this hunk of junk safe?'

He smiled and said, 'I hope so.'

And we took off into the blackness of the night. We sat there in silence, it was dark except for a small dim green glow from a small overhead light and the flash of a red light that blinked at thirty-second intervals. My mind was running the fifty-yard dash over and over. I kept coming back to the same question. Why the hell did I agree to this with no thought at all. Damn have I lost my mind?

I looked over at Doctor Swine and he looked as if he had fallen into a deep sleep. But he had a little eerie smile of satisfaction on his face.

When I looked back at Cindy, she was as white as a ghost and she was sitting up straight and stiff as a board with her hands placed palm down on her thighs. It looked like her fingers had a death grip on her legs. I remember it being very difficult to think straight. Hence the fifty-yard dashes of the mind.

The old helicopter was bouncing up and down. Then it would jerk from side to side with an awfully loud grinding noise that would make my stomach churn every time it ground the cogs together. I know it scared me shitless. But just to the left of me I could tell Cindy was far worse than I was. I watched her chest to see if she was still breathing because of the pallid look on her face. But with all the bouncing going on I could not tell for sure. At one point I could have sworn that we were so close to the surface of the ocean I heard and felt the waves slap the bottom of the aircraft. That's when I placed my hand on top of Cindy's hand. She slowly turned her face toward me and I stared into her beautiful bright blue eyes when they flashed into dark hallowed holes and she mouthed the words, 'WE WILL DIE.'

My heart sank as a wave of fear and emotions swept over me. When with a sudden jolt we were in a steep climb upward and a jolting stop of forward motion that the helicopter suddenly dropped about ten feet down to a grinding halt? That's when my mind screamed at me, we're crashing.

With cat like movement the doctor was up on his feet with a huge grin on his face. 'We have arrived!'

The cargo door then opened. As I unstrapped and stood up. I asked, 'are we not landing?'

With a sneaky grin, I really did not like the look on his face. 'Oh, no there's no room to land, it will be OK, trust me.'

I took Cindy by the arm to help her stand when the aircraft took another downward jolt that threw Cindy into my chest with a great force that nearly knocked us both crashing to the floor. luckily, I was able to grasp the crate with one hand. While using the other arm to grasp tightly around her waist to keep her from falling. I could feel her panic radiating through her breast into my chest. I held tight for a moment and told her it would be all right. I had no way of knowing if it would be OK or not, but the scent of her was captivating and I knew I had to say something.

There was another round of that awful grinding sound and the good doctor grabbed us by the arm to help us step up onto the platform that held the create. The sound of rattling chains and the grinding of gears and cogs was deafening. As the platform slid out the back of the helicopter, I was both terrified and excited. I struggled with my grip on Cindy as the doctor lowered us into complete blackness.

I sensed we were going down way farther than we should have gone from the look of the island, something was not right here plagued my mind as we continued downward in the blackness. All the time the sound of the helicopter was fading further and further away like the volume was being turned down. Suddenly with a loud thump we hit the bottom with a fierce jolt that rattled my teeth.

The area became flooded with light and a loud hum and a brilliant wave of light exploded into the room. For several moments, our eyes were blinded until they adjusted to the sudden brightness of light. Doctor Swine led us through a doorway into the living room area I have described earlier.

'I will show you to your quarters, so you can freshen up a little. Afterwards I will answer all your questions, fair enough?'

He led us down to the line of six little rooms.

'Man, this looks more like a fortress instead of a laboratory.'

'No worries Mr landing you will get to see the lab area in due time.'

We stopped at the first little room.

'This is your suite Mr landing. This suite right here is yours Miss Help-Land.'

'Wow, it sure isn't the Hilton!'

'I shall return for y'all after a while. Try to relax we will see each other soon.'

That's the last thing I heard before the door slammed shut. My heart sank as I heard the locks click into place. Through a small speaker the good doctor said, 'have no fear this facility has every room locked with a password-protected lock, it's all for your own protection. I should also point out that every room is soundproof so feel free to scream all you want.'

I stumbled backwards, half sat and half fell onto the small twin bed with my head spinning in loops.

Damn, Henry, what have you gotten yourself into. I sat trying to wrap my head around how quickly I had gotten into this mess. All I could do was to force myself to shake off that feeling of being trapped like an animal in a cage. I was awoken later with a slight foul smell in my nose. I bolted up to my feet. I heard the slight click of the speaker above the door. Damn he is listening to us. I could hear faint scuffling sounds. Then I heard Cindy cough all the while trying to scream. I really began to panic when I heard her body hit the floor then she was silent. Everything was silent.

'Doctor Swine, what's happening out there? Why are we locked in here? Hello.'

'All in good time, Mr Landing, all in good time,' came his voice from the speaker.

Then there was nothing. Now my fear is trying to get the best of me. No, I will not give up without a fight for what I want. Now there was nothing but silence Erie silence. Yet the screams in my mind are deafening. What could possibly be going on out there?

'Let me out of here now,' I screamed? I rushed to the door shoulder first only to bang my head on the floor. But still there was only the damn silence. The thoughts running through my head are mad. My childhood was so messed up, my parents were killed in a drunk driving accident when I was nine. The rest of my life had been bouncing from foster home to foster home. Stop it, Henry! Focus on this problem. You're trapped in a room and only God knows where we really are.

We must be somewhere in Mexico. Damn the silence is driving me crazy. Another round of, 'let me the fuck out here.'

Pacing back and forth to get hold of himself. You can think this through. OK, let's see, I left my doctor's at ten thirty yesterday morning with the news of terminal cancer. I spent four hours wandering the streets of Miami in a daze. Did I eat? How long has it been since I had eaten? Man, I am starving. Hey, can I get food while screaming and banging on the door. with only silence in return.

With my head hammering away, the thought of Cindy flooded my thoughts. We had only the briefest of encounters but the feel of her breast against my chest was like heaven. What happened to her, what will happen to me?' Random thoughts took over in their fifty-yard dashes with no logical thought. It has been many hours since I have heard a sound of any kind. How long has it been since we arrived here? Yet I have gotten no food or drink. Wait, I have not needed to go to the bathroom yet, that's got to be a bad thing. Dehydration must be close, is he going to leave me here to starve and thirst to death? Sleep crept up on me as I drifted off with my back against the door. My mind along with my body and my soul was extremely wasted.

I awoke startled with the feeling I was being strangled

I could not catch my breath. What the hell! I jumped to my feet, there was that foul smell again only this time it was much stronger. I can't breathe. It's getting foggy, what's happening? The last thing I remember clearly is that I was hitting the floor. I can feel the pressure of being dragged but I can't move, I can't talk, what is going on here? Suddenly I am hoisted on top of a steel table, face down. When I am awake, I can see the floor and the good doctor's shadow from the bright lights. But I am frozen in place. Oh God, I am paralyzed. Oh, what the hell! That's when he spoke.

'Hello Mr Landing I promised you I would explain everything.' Then a little chuckle comes out. 'Well, you see, Henry, I sort of misled you a little. I am a doctor, I was professionally until last year, you see my wife, oh how beautiful she is. Well, she got diagnosed with MRSA. It is a fatal skin disease that is eating her alive. Oh God, all the sores and scabs she has on her body right now. How in the world can a body as beautiful as hers ever produce that much puss? Anyway, sorry I was rambling there.

'So I came up with this brilliant plan to cure my wife. That's where you and Miss Cindy come in to play. Helen's doctor said there was no more they could do for her. But I beg to differ! I brought you and Miss Help-Land here so I could remove your skin and replace it on my wife's body. This way the new skin grafts will replace her skin. Taking the infected skin off and transplanting it with y'all's skin will save her life. You need not worry, Henry, I have no plans of killing you. And yes, I gave you a good gassing to put you under, that way there is no struggling. I gave you a gas form of anesthesia that I created. The anesthesia is a hypnotic general anesthesia. I had to change its contrast to create a gas form that would fill the room full, but it works well, as you can see for yourself. You will still be conscious and aware, so I know you can hear me, maybe even comprehend what I am saying. But you can't feel any pain. There's no way you can move or fight this way.

'I have removed most of the skin from your back already and you have not even flinched.'

In my head, I heard everything he was saying, but I was also building a fire of rage and hatred in my gut.

'OK, where was I, sorry I had to change to a thinner blade scalpel, the skin around the knees is delicate. Yes, so you feel no pain. It is quite a genius plan that keeps giving. I know you have terminal brain cancer, so you will however die. That I am sorry to say. I hate that fact, I really am not a monster after all, just a doctor trying to save my beloved wife. Hey, it's very time-consuming removing just four layers of skin in three-inch strips. But what the hell, it gives us time to talk. Are you still comfortable Mr Landing? Good! Glad to hear that you are coming around. It's always great to have happy patients. But the real beauty of this plan is I have developed an antiseptic mist I will apply to your whole body that does wonders for healing. Therefore, I will take four layers of skin from you then put you back in your room where you will get a daily gassing and the antiseptic misting. Lucky me, in five months I can pre-harvest your new skin again. Damn, is that not great, Mr Landing?

Here now let's roll you over so we can get to the other side now. There now, a change of scenery is always good. I bet by now you are wondering why I have selected you and Miss Help-Land for this project. That's simple, with a little research, thank God for Googling and yes, a brother-in-law that's a doctor too, you both are tall and have the same blood type as Helen, with you both having brain cancer your white blood cell count is way up, that helps the skin grafts take hold and fight the MRSA. So now I hope I have answered all your questions.'

By now I am lying on my back looking straight down my body screaming for him to stop.

But there is no sound coming out, just silence. With all the fear and panic and rage building up like a volcano inside me, I am forced to watch him cut and rip three-inch-wide strips of skin down my legs. Oh God, the sound of the ripping is now reverberating in my ears so loud, like the sound of a fine piece of cotton cloth being ripped in half.

'OK, Mr Landing, almost done are you still comfortable?'

'I hope you're still with me, you're not saying much. Even though the conversation was only a one-sided conversation, I think we have had the most enlightened chat this evening. All we have left to remove is the front of the arms and your chest. This is when he took my right arm into his hand, lifting my arm to his face for a closer look at it. Wow, Henry you have massive forearms this will produce great specimens.'

Boom! Like the force of a twenty-megaton nuclear bomb, the volcano exploded. Forty years of rage and hatred came crashing out of my right arm thrashing upward only a mere two inches or three my arm suddenly dropped like a rock striking the edge of the table and tumbled off the side. The weight of that dead arm suddenly snatched my body to the right. Hey, change of scenery is always good, right. Not for me, sad to say, the image I now have burned into my mind will haunt me forever as my eyes focused in on the now new scenery. There lay the good Doctor Swine crumpled on the floor with his throat slashed open blood gushing out in massive waves covering the floor a crimson color. What was even worse was the grin on his face. That grin of admiration he had while lusting over my forearm. It froze my body to the floor. You see, lying there staring at that grin for what seemed like hours, my mind was darting in and out of consciousness. Unable to move, waiting in the silence for the blackness to steal over me, it swallowed me deep within its black hole. I really remember only that. I awoke several hours later, no, maybe days later. I was in so much pain it is indescribable. I am trapped here in this locked and silent operating room, stranded on an island. Every door is password protected with no entry and no exits. The pain comes in waves now. When it comes, I am paralyzed till it passes, for sometimes hours. Doctor Swine removed three-quarters of my top four layers of skin. But I doubt I will live much longer. The infection has set in. I can feel the fever taking over my body. I do not understand how long I have been here now. Your guess would be as good as mine. I wanted to leave my story so that someday someone will know the truth of what really happened here. I found this journal and a pen to write with. I feel sure it has taken me a month, maybe more, to complete what I have written so far. Oh, shit, I feel the blackness coming again. Let this letter become known as my last words before the infection and my insanity kill me dead, all alone in the silence. Three good people died a horrible death here. But the good news is, there was one monster killed, now his troubled soul will forever burn in hell. PERDIDA MESA is once again uninhabited.

The End

THE LITTLE BLUE FLOAT

Tim Gibson's family made plans to float down the most popular stream in the small mountain town the next day. The day was a cool, crisp, July morning. With the water temperature twenty degrees cooler than the air, it will make for a chilly float. But Tim insisted they get an early start. He said it would warm up quick enough. Tim Gibson was an egotistical, arrogant, asshole. He usually got what he wanted by intimidating people with his size and bad temper.

    A friend had told him of an older Indian man that would provide them with floats for a lot less than the other float places and he would also show you a secluded place to float for a good way alone, therefore, Tim took down the old man's name and address. Earlier that day, as the sun was about to break the horizon Tim visited the old, Indian man about getting the floats. When he arrived, the man informed him that all the floats had left already. Tim had gotten irritated with the man from the start. Raising his voice, 'How the hell can you not have any when the sun is not fully up yet?' he asked.

    Tim lost his temper with the man. 'AJ told me you had floats for rent.' With every word his voice rose higher.

    The Indian man worried about his safety as this man seems to be loco. With catlike reflexes, Tim grabs him by the shirt. He pulls the man's face right to within kissing distance. 'I demand two adult floats and a child's float now, if not I will make your miserable life a living hell.'

'I don't have them right now, I can get them,' his voice was low and trembling. I believe it was the Indian man's first time in his eighty-six years that he felt fear for his life This white man was crazy, he could see it in his eyes.

'When? Dammit!' demanded Tim, 'when will you have them for me?' Shaking the man by his shoulders now.

He told Tim to come back around ten o'clock. 'When the moon has risen, I will have them.'

'Fine,' Tim shouted, showering the man's face with his spittle. Tim shoved him backwards, 'You better believe if you are fucking with me old man, I will fuck you up so bad.'

The old man shrugged his shoulders. 'Be back when the moon has risen,' and he turned and walked away.

As he walked away the old Indian man had a small sinister grin on his face. The old man knew deep in his heart how to deal with this crazy white man, 'Threaten me will you?' smiling as he watched Tim drive away.

Tim arrived back at the Indian man's house as the clock struck ten o'clock. Tim had already psyched himself up for a fight with this man. Tim always got his way. Tim felt surprised that there was no one around. The three floats stood up against a tree in front of the house. There were two bright red adult floats and a small little blue float. There was a sign hanging on them. Here are the floats you requested. They are free for you. Tim smiled, 'You're damn right they're free, I had to make two trips to get them. Damn, I had wanted to beat that son of a bitch for making me have to get rough with him. Oh well, I got the damn floats, anyway and the directions to the secret launching spot.

He took them and left. As he left the old Indian man

stood at the edge of the forest watching him by the light of the moon. He was chanting in a whisper.

Once Tim was home, he bragged to his wife. I told you! all you need is to persuade them a little.

Sandy Gibson just smiled. 'One of these days someone will persuade back. Then what are you going to do?'

'I will kick their fucking ass.' And he turned and strode off with chest stuck out like a bandy rooster.

The next morning Tim and his family was up and running at the crack of dawn. Sandy complained, 'It is too early Tim.'

'Oh, no it's not too early. We will have to get a jump on the other people. That way we have the stream all to ourselves. We can float down without being crushed by other tubers. Hey, come on get a move on woman.'

Tim stalked away. Sandy got Timmy up, so she could get him dressed.

He moaned, 'It's too early.'

Sandy replied, 'I know, son. I think we must go so your father does not get angry with us. You know how angry he can get. So, let's hurry the hell along and get ready. OK buddy?'

'OK, Mommy, he said with a smile. 'I have never floated down a creek. What is floating down creek going to be like, Mom?' little Timmy asked.

'It will be lots of fun, Timmy. All you do is sit down in the float and it will carry you downstream. Timmy's eyes lit up.

'Wow, kind of like the Indians did.'

'Yes, something like that.'

They were ready to go. Tim checked the tubes he had

tied to the top of the car. Had to make sure they were secure. They headed for the stream.

'It's only four miles to where they would put in,' Tim said. Once Timmy and Sandy were in their floats, he would tie them all together. 'That way we can stay together and no one floats away from the group.'

Sandy agreed that was a great idea. 'I am glad we get to do this, Tim, you work so hard for us we do not get to see you a lot.'

'You're right; I think this trip will be fun. AJ said it was a blast. He said it would be OK for Timmy to do. I checked the floats this morning. To make sure that crazy ass Indian had not sabotaged them.'

'Oh, I hope he didn't do that. It will be a great day with lots of fun and adventures.' Sandy took her husband's hand in hers. And she smiled.

Arriving at the launch site Tim parked the car and turning to his wife said, 'See I told you we would have it all to ourselves.'

'Yes, you did,' she replied. But what she wanted to say is that it was too cold for all the other people, that's why we are all alone. Not wanting to anger her husband, Sandy Gibson kept her mouth shut.

Tim untied the floats and he cursed and slapped the car twice when he had trouble untying the knots.

Tim Gibson was not a boy scout. Tim worked with great effort to get the floats off the car. From there he half carried, and half dragged them toward the edge of the stream. Struggling to carry all three floats Tim lost his footing and was soon lying flat of his back with his feet sticking up like an over-turned turtle.

Sandy tried, she tried so hard not to laugh, she almost peed herself. She did not want to laugh but she could not hold it in any longer. And she laughed. The laugh was short lived when Tim was suddenly on his feet like a cat. Sandy was almost knocked off her feet when her float struck her on the head.

'You want to laugh at me? Here, carry your own damn float.'

That's how mean Tim Gibson is.

Tim picked up the other two floats and walked the last five feet to the stream. Sandy stood there staring at him. Sometimes she loved and adored him with all her heart. Then there were times like this. He treated her like shit. In these times she often hated him to the point she could kill him. If looks could kill, Tim Gibson would have looked torn apart like a savage bear would rip apart another animal to protect her cubs.

Tommy broke her stare by asking, 'Are you OK, Mom?'

'Yes, sweetie I am OK, Daddy is just mean sometimes. Come on, let's have fun today.'

At the edge of the water, Tim was already stepping into the water. On the second step in the water he went to his knees. Tim let out a howl!

'Holy shit,' he cried out. 'Hurry the hell up Sandy so I can get out of this cold ass water.'

When Tim sat the little blue float down in the water, a sharp tingle shot through his entire body. He let go of the float. But he quickly grabbed it before it could get away. Damn must have been static electricity that got him he thought. It must have built up with the float rubbing against him as he carried them.

'Come on, sit down Tommy, I will hold it for you then I can hold your mother's while she sits in hers.'

Reluctantly, Sandy moved to the edge of the water.

'OK Tommy, all you must do is hold on, OK sweetie.

'Sure, Mom.' She picked him up and kissed him on the forehead. 'I love you, buddy.'

'I love you too, Mom.'

She sat him in the float's center.

The problem was, he did not just sit in the float he went all the way through. Suddenly Sandy was screaming with all her might. Startled, Tim reached out for her to see what was wrong. But he was too slow, suddenly Sandy Gibson and her son got sucked through the center of the little blue float.

'Sandy,' Tim yelled and grabbed up the float. He could see that both of them were gone to the bottom of the clear stream. Both his wife and son had disappeared. Stunned, Tim gripped the little blue float in his hand. He gripped it a little too hard and the wet, slippery float shot out of his hand and it hit him right square in the face. The blow caused the float to pop up in the air. Tim could do nothing, the float came down on his head and as he disappeared, the sound of crunching bones echoed in the stillness, the little blue float hit the water in a bloody whirlpool. Somewhere off in the distance there was a faint laughter.

In the cool, crisp, July morning, the little blue float began its slow trip down the stream. It bobbled up and down on the trickling stream. A quarter of a mile downstream, a large elk walked up to the edge of the stream to get a drink of the cool water. As he drank the water, he thought it tasted heavenly this morning. The elk's mouth was dry from his long night's sleep and he needed the water. The elk was in a deep blissful state when the little blue float bumped into his nose. The elk had not even had time to raise his head before his head, up to his shoulders, was through the center of the little blue float. The elk's back legs shot out pushing the little blue float out deeper into the stream. Half of the little blue float was under water with the weight of the elk. If you had been standing near the float, it would have sounded like someone squeezing a wad of bubble wrap. The front legs and the ribs of the elk were being crushed and crumbled as the elk slid through center of the little blue float and out of sight. The sight of it would have driven you mad. watching the elk melt away into thin air through center of the float.

The sun was brightening more and more, burning off the morning fog of the smoky mountains. Sam Wiggins was a retired widower. He came out to the stream every morning to trout fish. Sam was a fifth-generation fly fisherman. To him fly-fishing was the only fishing there was. This morning his luck was in stride. He already had two of his five bag limit within the first hour and he was approaching his honey hole. Sam tied on his favorite fly, a brown hackle with a yellow stripe. This fly always worked in the honey hole. Sam stood up straight, spread his legs to a comfortable position. He took a deep breath and blew it out in a rush. he was taking in the rumbling sound of the water. He raised the fly out of the water. Slinging his arm backward to make his favorite hackle fly like the wind, only it did not fly, just as his arm reached the farthest point of his backward stroke something bumped his leg. It startled him into a frenzy. The fly string flew from his hand sending his favorite fly up into the nearest tree. Stumbling to keep his balance, he put his hand out to steady himself. While he held onto his rod in the other hand. Only his hand did not touch water, it touched smooth plastic. In an instant his eyes caught sight of what had hit his leg. As Sam was being folded up like a single slice of bread into the center of the little blue float. He was looking between his legs trying to scream. His mind registered what was happening, 'Shit, I am being eaten by a little blue float.' There was only silence as the little blue float drifted away downstream leaving a faint red streak in the water.

It was now two hours after the Gibson family first sat in the little blue float in the water. Ted Gambrell and his wife, Doris, were staying in a small cabin right on the edge of the stream. They had just come out onto the porch for their morning ritual of coffee and cigarettes. As Ted sat down, he noticed the little blue float hung up on a stump bobbing up and down at the rippling water's edge.

'Hey, Doris, look at that, some kid lost his float,' Ted remarked.

'Wow,' Doris said. 'I hope the kid that lost it is OK. Come help me get it out of the water I do not want to see it get popped on a tree limb and therefore litter up the creek bank.'

With a grumble, muttering under his breath, Ted got up. 'Damn man can't even have his coffee without having to work.'

'Quit your bellyaching and come on.'

At the edge of the water, Doris reached out to grab the little blue float. It was just out of reach of her fingertips.

'Here, Ted, take my hand, that way I can step out a little further.'

So, Ted took her hand in his, careful not to squeeze too hard. Doris leaned out further this time, she could barely place her hand on the thing to drag it closer. As her hand tighten on the float, her eyes suddenly widened as a black hole opened up inside the little blue float. Then she was being sucked in. The sudden jolt of his wife's body being snatched forward caught Ted off-guard.

Suddenly his wife's body was up to her waist inside the little blue float. Ted's foot slipped with the weight of his wife. His right foot left the bank and plunged into the water he lost his grip on her hand. When he was a foot from the bank, Ted reached out as he fell backwards, reaching out he could grab Doris's foot. With Ted's weight pulling backwards he pulled Doris's body backwards also. He thudded against the bank hard enough to knock the breath out of him. As he opened his eyes, he saw his wife's upper torso it had all the flesh ripped off. Her guts and intestines strung out like spaghetti going into the center of the little blue float. He screamed, and his body was then jerked forward, and Ted's world went black as he plunged head-first into the little blue float. The little blue float moved downstream. There was a string of intestines hanging off the side of the float. Suddenly and quietly the intestines string sucked out of sight into the center of the float just like you suck in a string of spaghetti.

Just outside of the town a young couple was standing on a bridge. They were looking down into the water. They were holding hands and making plans to get married in the fall. When out from under the bridge the little blue float drifted into their line of sight silently floating. Hey, look at that float they both said at the same time. Someone lost their float. Laughing the young man pointed down the river. Just around that bend is the city park where the stream splits. And today they have that fishing derby for the kids. there will be a hundred kids out there. I am going guess that some lucky kid will get a new little blue float.

While on the other side of town an old, Indian man sat on his porch. He had a wide grin on his face. He was in a trance-like state, mumbling a chant unbroken by the silence. Meanwhile, the little blue float floated on toward the city park's fishing derby.

The End

THE FADING

My name is Joan Walker known by my Cherokee name as Eagle Raven, ruler over the sky, day and night. I write this as the cancer is devouring my innards. It will not be long before I will drift on the breeze with the eagles. I have lived with this story, or nightmare you could say, in my heart keeping it cold and black. Now I will reveal my darkest secrets of The Fading.

My grandmother was the daughter of a Cherokee medicine man. At fifteen she had gotten raped. the rapist was Jonathan a youthful college student that had showed up in the village one day. His goal was to make a report on the traditions of the Cherokee customs. He had lived among them for four days asking many questions and making notes in his journal. On the fourth day, just as the sunlight was fading away into the western sky; he requested that my grandmother accept his invitation for a stroll with him down by the stream. While they were all alone, and out of sight and out of earshot, he put a piece of tape over her mouth and dragged her into the underbrush. There he molested her.

Her screams now obscured behind the tape as he shredded her insides apart with his enormous member. She not only bled from being a virgin but from the tearing of her tissue inside her from his savage thrusting. She would never forget his awful grin and the expression of triumph in his eyes. Grandmother told me his eyes reflected the look of a beast. The images would always remain sealed in her mind.

When he had finished raping her, he reached down and took a large rock and struck her on the side of her head with brutal force. That's when he escaped leaving her for dead and disappeared forever. Sure, many of the tribe's braves ensued in pursuit, but they never encountered him or the path which he used to escape. My grandmother lived on the outskirts of the village with my mother. They are being treated like outsiders by the other villagers. Supposedly, my grandmother had helped him to get away. Since he disappeared ever so swift and untraceable. several warriors from the village searched for him for several days. But I am here to inform you that the rumor is not accurate.

At sixteen, my mother went into the big metropolis of Ashville with a Christian church group she had been taking part in. When she arrived back, she had become pregnant with me. They coerced her into having sex with one young church member. When I was three my mother had been so severely humiliated by other villagers, she took her own life as her way of escaping the torment she incurred. A tale that's spoken around the village spread the news we had received a curse by the whole incident. So now my grandmother and I had no one else. We were being shunned from the village as an outcast.

I was seven years old when my grandmother made me aware of the talent I had gained. She noticed me sitting in the doorway, Indian style, motionless, when I had not responded to her to calling out my name; she rushed over placing her hand on my shoulder and her touch forced me back to my body. Shocked at the sight of her that a slight scream escaped me which caused my grandmother to scream.

'You startled me,' I blurted out.

'You had me terrified, first you were sitting there motionless and would not acknowledge my calling for you.'

'Sorry, Grandma, I was strolling with the hound.'

Grandma's eyes shot open wide as she demanded, 'Whatever do you mean, you were strolling along with the hound?'

'I can walk with the animals then,' Joan shrugged her shoulder as if to express it's no big deal.

'Please explain your secret,' Grandma burst out, now her face was glowing with enthusiasm.

'Well, I can insert my mind inside the animal's mind then I can see what they see. I can understand what they feel. Like the hound I was just walking with, I could feel the starvation in his abdomen I could feel his desolation. Then could feel the agony in his rear hip where a small lad had previously shot him with a slingshot for fun. Best of all I can converse with them only while I was fading.'

Stunned, 'When did you learn that you had the ability?' Grandma asked?

'From the eagle, he spoke to me and I met with him and the raven. They explained what I needed to do to fade. I do not just become inside them, it feels like a fading shadow. Dim at first and then it gets brighter. I cherish the time I get to fly with the eagle. You can almost see the entire world from up there. And you're not frightened that you want come back to your body. With only using my mind to think of my body I am instantly returned into my body. I also now know if my body is touched, I will return.'

'Has my father taught you about the ability to do this

out-of-body experiment? My grandmother asked. 'Who showed you how?'

'A couple years ago, the eagle told me. He and I sat and talked for hours. Atlas the eagle said I should not speak of it to anybody. He said it was a legacy given to me from our forefathers, from a long time ago.'

They remained seated in the doorway for a long while just peering at each other, before Joan broke the silence. 'You will not mention this to anyone, will you Grandma? I want no one else to learn what I can do.'

'Oh, no child, your secret's safe with me.'

I went on using my fading talent over the next few years working on progressing up to larger game animals like deer and elk. It is an incredible feeling to stroll through the woodlands in the mind of a large deer. You can feel the awesome power of its muscles as it strolled along. grazing on young delicate leaves. Moving among the underbrush noiseless moving along without a care in the world. Even though it was a large, graceful deer, its instincts warned him to pause here and there occasionally to sniff the air. oh, man how crisp the deer's sense of smell was, everything he smelled. It seemed enhanced by a hundred-fold. Inside the deer it was like a daydream, you appeared like you were hovering above the eyelids.

It happened on an early November morning I was in the forest walking around taking in the forest's elegance relishing the cool crisp air that was filling my lungs. I heard the noise of the crack of a stick. Startled, I had a very frightening feeling creep into my bones. I scurried behind a large oak tree. That's when I saw a young native American boy emerge from the underbrush with his bow and arrow slung over his shoulder. He clambered out into the corner of this small clearing. The clearing was tiny. It was maybe ten foot in width. There were several young trees at its boundary with deer rubs scarring their bark. He saw the area would produce an excellent hunting place. He squatted down and he placed his back to a tree just out of sight of the clearing.

But from my vantage point I could see him clear as a bell. I could sense his dread. It radiated off him in powerful waves. As I observed him, I wondered why he appeared so miserable and concerned at the same moment. Maybe it was his first hunt alone to prove his manhood. During the moment of an instant fear, despair, and worry struck me with such great pressure it tried forcing me to scream, but nothing would come out, then the blackness overcame me. Joan thus understood she had faded into this lad. She had never considered the ability to fade into another living individual. The feeling was so extraordinary. I learned how to walk down on all four legs as the animals. This feeling was awkward being upright inside him it was also unnerving at first. I had to adapt my mind to collect control to keep my stability. After the confusion of fading into this boy subsided, I saw his memories and it all came clear at once. Feeling all these emotions pulsing out of him like an exploding volcano. This was his first hunt. His father had gotten killed in a riding accident three months previously.

He and his father were riding a pathway through the forest when Teko, that is his name, had seen the serpent at the same instant the mare felt the threat. She reared up throwing his father off. Teko watched in slow motion as his father's head struck a rock jutting out from the ground at the side of the pathway. His father's head cracked open like a ripe melon before his eyes. At that moment Joan slammed back into her own body with such force she skidded to the ground, crumpling at the base of the tree she was standing behind. Stunned and perplexed she sat up; her heart was aching for this boy now compelled to perform as a man of the house at such an early age. All at once it occurred to her. An idea how she could help relieve the anxiety he has inside him.

    I can fade into a nice buck and perhaps convince him to wander into the clearing. Teko can get the meat his family required. He was now providing for his mother and three younger sisters as well the rest of the tribe. They could only survive if everyone pitched in to hunt. As Joan prepared to fade, she could fade into the animal from as far away as a mile. she needed only to focus her mind on the animal she meant to fade into, then she was seeing through the eyes of a massive thirteen-point buck. Her vision blurry at first but quickly cleared. The deer knew in an instant of his purpose. It accepted the fate that was being requested of him. He twisted around and headed in the direction of the clearing. The buck made his approach into the meagre clearing with no reluctance. He marched forwards eager to please the god inside his head. He gave his life up so other younger life can grow up and prosper.

    When the deer was a hundred yards from the clearing, Joan could feel the fear creeping into his heart. His heart violently raced in his rib cage. She did her best to sooth the deer with increasing words of praise to him. At that moment she faded back to her body. Then she faded into Teko. She so wanted to feel his emotions as he got the satisfaction from accomplishing his duty to his family. He was on his feet. He had his arrow already knocked into the bowstring. While, as the bowstring drew backwards all thoughts left his mind, the only thing that remained was a phrase repeating over and over. Aim with your heart. The deer stepped into the clearing his head was hanging down. Teko's heart leaped in his chest. He whispered the words out loud, aim with your heart. He then released the bowstring. The arrow flew true, hitting its mark with a clean heart shot. The buck fell onto his side, dead. The last thought on the buck's mind was of a cool brook flowing gently.

Teko's emotions went wild. Joan struggled to keep up with them. Joy, loss, excitement grateful and sadness all at once. Joan faded out. Once back in her own body she felt exhausted, but also wonderful too. She had used her talent to benefit someone other than herself. That made her feel wonderful. When she stood up and peeked around the tree, she saw Teko saying a prayer to the gods for their gift to him and his family. I watched in silence as he tried to pull the deer with all his mite. But it would not move. It had to outweigh him by a hundred sixty pounds. I stepped out from behind the tree.

'Hello, I am Joan, nice shot there.'

Teko, although pulling with all his might, let go, he then stumbled off his feet. falling to the ground with a thud. I had to giggle I could not hold it back. He stood up glaring at me with amazement.

'Are you OK?' I asked.

Embarrassed, he stood up, 'Yes you startled me.'

'I am sorry. I did not mean to startle you so bad. I

wanted to offer my help to you in dragging your kill, but only to the edge of the village, you will have to get other help from there.

With a trembling voice Teko said. 'You are the girl that lives with her grandmother on the edge of the village.'

'Yes, that is me. My name is Joan.'

'I have always heard to stay away from your house and to not talk to you or your grandmother.'

'I heard the same tale as well. But you need help with the deer and I can provide that help. We don't even have to talk just pull our weight. With a shrug of his shoulders, he agreed to allow her to help him. Taking one of the back legs together they dragged the deer in a slow steady pace. Heavy underbrush forced them to take the long two-mile path back to the edge of the village where I bid him well and walked back into the forest. I was busting with excitement to tell my grandmother the story of what had happen.

When I had returned home, my grandmother was not there, very disappointed I went to my room and dropped across the bed exhausted. I was soon fast asleep. When I awoke my room was now dark as midnight. I rush out to share my adventure with my grandmother. When I arrived in the kitchen, it surprised me to see she was not there. The kitchen was empty. I started for the living room when I heard the faint squeak of her back-porch rocker. I came busting out the back door full of excitement to speak with my grandmother. When I saw the look on her face, I stopped cold in my tracks. Grandmother what is wrong. She raises up her hand in a stopping motion. I could see the fury rising in her cheeks.

'I have told you many times before not to be around the

other villagers. Now you have disobeyed my orders, by helping that young boy drag a deer back to the village today.'

'But Grandmother you don't understand what happened. I had to help him drag it I am so sick of being an outcast. I have done nothing wrong,' I screamed. 'Why am I being punished for something that happened sixty years ago?'

'I hate it. I hate it.' I then stormed off the porch and ran straight into the forest. I was furious and upset with my grandmother I needed to be alone. And the forest is my playground. Once in the tree's shelter. I paced back and forth.

'I don't understand why I have to be an outcast? When I have done nothing wrong to anyone. I have visited none of the other villages in my life. Damn I am sick and tired of being called an outcast. Is there a way to fix this? There must be,' I screamed into the darkness.

I had been walking in circles for quite a while before I sat down on a fallen tree. My head was spinning. When I took in a breath of the cool crisp air, I thought of Teko. Teko had nothing to do with this mess I'm sure of it? The thought came into my mind in a flash. Therefore, I stood straight up as if I had hit a brick wall. In an instant I had faded into Teko, another human.

I sat down with a grunt. 'How was it possible to fade into Teko? This time I said it out loud?

I know now what to do. my face was beaming I could feel it rising in my cheeks. I had a smile from ear to ear. If I could fade into Teko, I could fade into someone else. I could see their memory's. Grandmother! I can finally find out what happen to her. After I know what happened, then I can begin to find a solution to get us unbanned from the village. She will never tell me the truth of what happened. I will wait till she goes to sleep and then I will find out the truth of what happen. Therefore, if I know the truth, I can find out how to fix it. Joan smiled in the darkness.

OK, now I had a plan, and I meant to execute it tonight. I have had a long nap, I am wide awake. At this hour it is the best time to do it before I lose my nerve. With my plan in place, I headed back to the house. I hated the thought of facing my grandmother, not until she knew the truth. Upon returning to the porch my grandmother said something I could not hear. So, I did not give her a chance to get started in on me, shaking my head, no and walking right past her into the house. Flopping onto the bed I was feeling excited and scared all at the same time. My emotions were running rampant in my head. my whole time as a little girl I desired to know what had happen to my grandmother yet, at the same time I am feeling like a thief. The whole idea of what I intended to try would be like breaking into my grandmother's memories. Her cat burglarious heart told her it was wrong to do this thing she was planning to do. It is so wrong by all the God's rules. Someway I will find out the truth I have too. Deep inside my soul I can feel that soon the truth of what happened will truly reveal everything then maybe there is a way to right the wrong. I want to free us from this curse.

I threw myself down on the bed where I cried till I had no more tears left. I cried for me. I cried for my mother. And I cried for my grandmother. We have experienced persecution long enough it is time for a change. When she had cried out all of her tears, she whispered to the darkness It's late I must do it now.

Grandmother is asleep by now. In an instant everything went black. Thank the Gods the blackness is only of the briefest moment. I guessed it's the moment I leave my body. Peaceful black bliss. Slam, my body was being crushed with agony and pain like nothing I had ever felt before. Sadness along with misery. Then I could not breathe. Feeling hurt and dying from the pain in my head. I had become thrust back into my room. Lying on the bed my body convulsing in violent spasms. I slowed down the convulsing till they became just shivers. There had been a long time span before I could become coherent enough to know where I was. I found myself curled into the fetal position. my arms throbbed in pain from having them wrapped around my chest in a death grip. There was pain everywhere throughout my body, even in my brain. That's when the panic set in. Oh my god, my brain will explode. I have succeeded in killing myself this time I panicked.

I had slowed my sobs to sniffles as I sat up. My head was clearing. Oh, my God I thought. Oh, my what had happened? Funny nothing like this, shocking and as powerful has happened when I faded in the past. Then I thought of Teko. How I had felt his pain and sorrows. My God, my grandmother must be in tremendous agony over what has happen. I arrived at the conclusion it was her destiny to find out what has happened to her grandmother. My will power took over, and I faded into my grandmother. The pain was the most shocking that caused her body to shake and convulse. Every part of her grandmother's body ached. It was so hard to breathe as my grandmother took shallow ragged breaths into her tired old lungs.

I gained control, fighting to shut out the pain in my mind as I searched through my grandmother's memories. With thousands of memories, it was overwhelming. Searching for hours before what I was looking for shot out at her. I could see the face of a young man as it rushed out like a photo from a distance. Then it enlarged itself as it made its way toward me. Once the image was face to face. the image rocked her little mind like the ground shaking at the bottom of a volcano just before erupting. Fearing for my life I was helpless.

Then the eruption happened, it slammed me to the ground. I hit so hard it knocked the breath out of me. Then I felt a hand on my mouth squeezing hard enough to pierce my lips with my teeth. I tasted the blood as it trickled down my throat. I knew my grandmother was reliving the memory. I had become horrified but the pull to know the truth would not let me fade out. I was in her mind and all she could feel and understand became a tornado in her head. She felt her dress being ripped from her body. Then his mouth was upon her breast. Sucking hard sending sharp pains through her chest. She was pinned she could not move.

Pain, oh God the pain in the place between her legs was being ripped apart she felt the flesh and maybe the tissue tearing like you would rip a piece of paper. I could feel the blood gushing out of her as his massive prick penetrated her private place. All she did was stare wide eyed into his face. The face that would always burn inside her mind forever. The second thrust of his prick felt as if in hit her in the throat from the inside she then lost consciousness.

I awoke screaming. The foul stench of his breath still lingered in my nostrils. The taste of blood coating my lips and throat. I trembled with the fading pain throughout my whole body. I had also wet myself sometime through the whole ordeal. I sat up straight as my grandmother entered my room.

'Are you OK dear? Was it a nightmare that had you screaming?'

'Yes, it was,' I said through the sobs pouring out of her as she investigated her grandmother's haggard, worried face. After using great effort, I was able to not reveal what I had done the night before. I wanted to tell. If I did, it would break the thin thread that was holding the relationship between me and my grandmother together. I knew deep in my heart it was my responsibility to do this on my own. All alone.

I stood up on shaky legs I could still the faint pain between my legs as I walked over to my grandmother, 'Everything will fine, I love you, Grandmother.'

'I love you too child. I am sorry I jumped on you about talking to that boy. It pains my heart to know you are shut off from the rest of the village. I would give anything to fix the trouble that plagues us with the villagers. But I cannot do that, and your mother tried, and it cost her her life. The information would have been more than a young child at your age to bear. For all I know it's a curse we will have to die with my child.'

'I cannot accept that, Grandmother. Somehow there must be a way to locate that demon bastard and bring him back here to face his crimes.'

'What did you say, Joan?' She reached out to take my

arm, but I was too fast, I stepped backward. Fear was trying to freeze me in place. Although the need to fix things became more powerful than the fear, turning around I ran for the door.

'Oh God, Joan, what have you done. Joan, you come back here! Don't go out that door we need to discuss this matter.' Grandmother muttered under her breath, 'hard headed child just like her mother.'

'I heard my grandmother scream as the door slammed shut. My mind was racing. Now what am I going to do. I cannot believe I let my emotions get the best of me.

'Oh God, Grandmother will be so irate with me. I was feeling faint as I made my way into the forest. There I felt at home and safe with the animals.

Once I was in the forest, I stumbled and fell into a large bunch of roots sticking out of the ground. When I fell between them, I fainted from exhaustion. And there I laid entangled in the roots. I awoke with a ragged scream at the slight touch of a soft smooth hand on my neck. It was on my jugular vein to be precise. Little known to me as I tried to jump up, I was then slammed back to the ground.

'I will not harm you. It appears your hair is tangled in the roots.'

I could not understand what was happening. Was he going to hurt me like my grandmother got hurt? Then my head was free to move. So, move I did, I scrambled up close to the next tree over.

'Please don't hurt me,' I said through a trembling voice. meanwhile saying this with a look of fear and a beautiful sound in my voice. That just broke Teko's heart.

'Joan it's me, Teko, I am not going harm you. That I

give you my word and honor on.'

I trembled like a scared rabbit. I raised my head up and behold, right before my eyes, I was looking deep into his eyes, they were as blue as the ocean. Along with a smile as wide as the Grand Canyon. My heart leaped up into my throat. I was hot with blush now.

'Hi,' I squeaked out.

'I am not supposed to be talking to you…' They spoke in unison. They both laughed out loud.

'You first,' I said motioning toward him with one of my trembling hands.

'OK. I sure got my hide tanned for allowing you to assist me with the deer the other day. But it was worth it to talk to you. For some strange reason I feel as if you had more to do with the large buck coming right next to me.'

At this statement my expression cause Teko to recoil back from me.

'You had something to do with it. I knew it wow. How? Please tell me how I knew my feelings were right, you are pure goodness. you are an angel from the gods.'

At this sudden turn of events, I had become stunned to silence. I was shocked and amazed at how quickly he had figured out I intervened in his hunt.

I snapped back to reality at the sound of his sweet soft voice.

'Are you OK? I am sorry if I have offended you?' He had the total look of fear on his face.

'Oh no, you have not offended me at all, you are my savior you saved me from the roots.'

I smiled not only on my lips but all over my body. I instantly felt safe with him. somehow, I knew I trusted him with all my heart. And that he felt the same way. There was a total merging of their minds along with their hearts and souls. They both fell into each other's arms on the ground beneath the large oak tree. Their bodies convulsed and it felt as if lightning was dancing between their bodies. The emotions and memories were swirling between them in massive jolts of electricity. Meer moments passed by before the two of them knew everything about the other. Then they drifted off to sleep from pure exhaustion.

After, they slipped into a deep sleep, their arms embracing the other, later they awoke, it had been several hours and each one of them felt great. When they both awoke with a smile on their face Teko spoke first, 'Oh my gods what happened?'

'I believe we became one with each other. My grandmother has taught me many of the old ways even though the village banned us. I remember her talking about that when two people become one with each other they are bound as one forever.'

Teko bore a shocked look on his face! Teko asked, 'Is that true?'

Smiling I said, 'I think so, I can feel your heart beating right next to mine. Can you not feel it in your chest?'

Amazed he put his hand over his chest, 'Yes, I can feel two heartbeats. Oh, the gods, my mother is going to tan my hide now oh,' and he slid down the tree in a wobbly fashion. How could this happen?

'I am not sure about that Teko. All my life till now I have never felt so much love for anyone as I do for you.' As I said these powerful words, I continued to look him straight into his eyes.

'I feel the same Joan I really do, but I don't understand how I know everything about you, everything.'

'Well, I guess that's what it means to be as one,' she said with a smile. 'Now I know everything about you too.'

After the thought occurred to him Teko blushed and turned his head away. Suddenly he turned back to her. 'What is this fading you do? I know you can do it, I cannot understand what it is you can do.'

'It started out I was just fading into animals. I can fade into one and it is as if I am that animal. I can feel what they feel, I see from their eyes. I can also whisper suggestions to them in their mind. that's what I did to the large deer you shot.

'You were the first person I ever faded into and all I did was whisper steady in your mind, so you would relax and make a great shot. I am sorry I did not understand I could fade into a person until you. And with you, it was as if your power dragged me into you, it all happened so fast. Well. That's when I faded into my grandmother and found out why we were so cursed. When she found out we got in a huge fight and I ran out. Then you found me under the tree.'

'Heaven forbid, we must find this man and return him to the village. Then the elders can punish him and the curse on me and my grandmother get broken.'

With eyes as wide as saucers I asked, 'OK, how are we going to find him, we know what he looks like when he was young, but he has changed with age?'

'Maybe so, but if I can get close to him, I can sense him. I can also tell from his aura I went through the rape as she did. It was so real I can still feel the soreness from it.'

'I know it sounds crazy, but it's the truth.'

Just then a single tear trickled down her cheek. He leaned over and kissed it away with his soft gentle lips. 'I know Joan, I believe you. I can feel the truth in you. OK what do we need to do? Any idea of which direction we need go to find this vile man?'

'Well, he told the village chief he was from the college in Ashville. But how do we get there?'

Teko brightened, 'I have a pack ready. I was going on a hunt tomorrow. I'll get it and meet you back here in an hour.'

'OK, great, see you back here. Be careful Teko don't get caught. I want to be right back.'

Once Teko stepped into the underbrush, I faded into a large rabbit nearby and urged it to follow Teko. I now felt responsible for his life. Not only was he a part of me now, I cared for him deeply, in fact I loved him.

I followed close behind him, the bunny was a silent creature, stealthily following. Suddenly he came to the clearing. Teko strolled across the clearing. I and the bunny stopped right inside the clearing. I could hear a dog. I could hear its breathing in my head. However, I could not see a dog, but I knew it was close. So there at the edge of the clearing I waited and watched for Teko to return. I could not believe how quickly things were moving. Wow, maybe I can break the curse. And then I hoped my grandmother would not be angry with me. Deep in my thoughts when Teko almost stepped on me and the bunny. The bunny scrambled into the underbrush giving Teko a fright, the bunny stopped at a little scream that escaped him. Then it jolted off back to where I was to meet him.

Teko arrived back to the large oak tree there he found

me sitting on a root smiling at him. He gave me a shy smile. Did you enjoy your stroll with the rabbit? he asked.

Blushing, I asked, 'How did you know I had faded into the rabbit? I was following you. I could feel you near me. I could feel my love burning for you.'

At this I had revealed the secret, my face began blushing a bright red.

'Anyway, I told my mother I was leaving earlier because I was having to go a little further out to find the bigger game. I also told her I would stay a couple of extra days, so I could pack extra food without a bunch of questions asked.'

'That was smart, Teko, I am impressed.'

Now it was Teko's turn to blush. 'OK let's head out, we need to head south-east of where we are.'

'OK I will follow you.' And with that the pair headed off hand in hand.

We walked in silence for almost two hours. We seemed to communicate in our heads. I found out he loved his two younger sisters with all his heart. And his mother he also felt bad for deceiving her this afternoon. I felt bad for him. he has sacrificed a lot for me all in one day. It was nearing dusk when Teko stopped and set the pack down.

'This is the place we will need to make camp for the night. It is getting dark. I will grab the wood we will need for a fire. There is a pot in the pack if you will grab water.'

'Sure, and we worked well together. We got a fire started and while Teko set up a lean-to I fixed the rabbit stew.

After eating it was now fully dark, the small fire gave off little light. When suddenly there was the sound of a large stick cracking. In an instant Teko was up on his feet with his bow in hand. I couldn't believe how quick and effortless he was to protect me. I stood and placed my hand on his arm and whispered it is OK if he wants to harm us.

Just then a very large wolf stepped among us. It was just about four feet high. Teko trembled at the sight of his large teeth. His huge eyes seemed to bore right through him.

It dropped to its belly and crawled over to my feet laying its snout on top of my foot. It seemed to Teko that it was grinning as I scratched his head.

Smiling I said, 'It's OK, you can pet him, also you are now a part of me.'

Reluctantly Teko reached out and stroked the great wolf on the head. it was so soft and fury. It felt like a bunny's tail.

'Don't worry Teko he is here to protect us, as long as I can remember he has always been close by, always right next to me when I was out after dark, lurking in the shadows.'

'That's right, I remember now you have this gift with the animals. Yes, something like that.

The fire was dying, so we both crawled into the lean-to with the wolf lying in the entrance to the lean-to. We are soon fast asleep. We awoke the next morning to the sound of the stream falling over some rocks. It was the most soothing sound, you must love the sound of running water. Other than the bright sunlight peeking through the trees. Teko noticed that the wolf was no longer guarding the entrance to the lean-to.

We got up feeling wonderful. We both felt full of life. I grabbed fresh water as Teko packed up the lean-to back inside the pack. They smiled at each other as they ate a hunk of dried deer jerky for breakfast. After they had gotten moving again, I asked,

'How do you know we are heading in the right direction? It's strange that we have seen no other signs of life in a long time.'

'My father told me this stream turned into a large river that flowed through Ashville all the way to the ocean. If we stick close to the stream it should take us right into Ashville.'

As we walked, Teko took my hand.

'I am so glad fate brought us together.'

Smiling, I leaned over and kissed him, 'Me too,' I whispered against his lips. 'Me too.'

The air had become warm, but it was cooler down by the stream. Around one we stopped for some lunch. This time we had dried fish to eat.

'Have you any idea how long it will take us to reach Ashville?'

'We have been making good time. I think we should arrive sometime tomorrow.'

After eating we sat down next to a large tree growing near the water's edge. talking about how beautiful this area was down by the stream. It was so peaceful and quiet. The birds were singing beautiful melodies, the soothing sound of the water had us both drifting off, in the warm lazy afternoon sun.

Suddenly the peaceful tranquility became shattered by a loud roar. Startled awake by the sound, Teko shoved me behind him as he was suddenly face to face with the largest bear he had ever seen. Teko could feel his hot stinky breath blasting him in the face. His life flashed before his eyes.

Teko realized there was no time to reach for his bow the bear was too close, snarling with a mouth full of razor-sharp teeth.

Teko feared he was about to die but all he could think of was to protect me even if it meant to sacrifice his own life.

Just then the bear roared and stood on his hind legs to attack. That gave Teko the moment he needed to grab his knife from the sheath. It may slash me to pieces but maybe I can stab it before it can get to Joan, he thought. The massive bear stood seven foot tall. As it took two steps toward Teko, he raised the knife to retaliate.

From out of nowhere there was a large thud next to them. It shook the ground beneath them. With a vicious snarl the wolf appeared shoving his shoulder into the bear's ribcage. The impact easily slammed the bear to the ground. Teko saw his chance and when the pair hit the ground Teko pounced stabbing the bear in the heart. The bear wailed in agony. Teko stabbed again as the wolf tore at his throat. Then all was silent. Except for the sound of the stream.

I, gasping for air, ran over to Teko now pinned to the ground by the bear's front arm and head. With the wolf pulling on the head and me pulling on the arm finally Teko could slide free. I hugged him so hard. Then I was shaking him like a rag doll, don't you ever scare me like that again ever. Then I was hugging him again. The wolf dropped his head and started off up the stream. That's when Teko stood up, 'Hey wolf', he spoke with a gentle tone.

The wolf stopped and turned toward him, 'Thank you,' Teko said with a bow. With a nod of his head the wolf turned and trotted off.

Suddenly Teko was in front me taking my hand. Please forgive me it was so peaceful I drifted off to sleep. If I had not fallen asleep, the bear would have not gotten so close to us.'

'Oh, my dear Teko there is nothing to forgive. You put your life in front of that bear for me. I owe you my life. My love for you is only growing stronger and stronger for you. You are my knight in shining armor. I pulled him to his feet to face me. There I kissed him passionately. Thank you for everything.'

'What do you need to do with the bear now that he is dead.' I asked?

'Well, we must skin it and remove the guts, so the meat won't spoil. We can then pack the meat with wet leaves and cover it with sand here near the edge of the stream. It will keep for a few days. There is enough meat there for both our families to have meat for months.'

'OK, but I have never skinned anything on my own before I have seen it done therefore, I intend to do my best to help,' I said with a smile.

That smile of mine warmed Teko all the way to his toes.

So, we skinned the bear and then dug out a hole in the sand big enough for the bear to lie in. We gathered large leaves dunking them in the stream and then lined the bottom and the sides of the hole with them. Teko had to cut the bear in half, we could not move the whole thing at once it was too heavy. Once it was in the hole, we packed more leaves on top of it. Teko was careful to only cut a large hunk of meat off and lay it aside. Smiling he said, 'Dinner tonight.' By the time we had covered it with sand it was late in the evening. I got fresh water and Teko built a fire. While he was looking for wood, he found a ginger root which he sliced and stuffed into slits in the bear meat. As the meat cooked our mouths watered. With the smell of roasted meat, and the roasted ginger root it blended together to make a beautiful aroma that hung all through the air.

When Teko got up to turn the meat he noticed two large yellow eyes just past the edge of the firelight. With that he knew that their friend was back in town. Their guardian angel. 'Come on boy,' Teko said, 'you deserve meat as much as we do.' And then there he was laying down at Teko's feet. The wolf rolled over exposing his underside to Teko in submission.

'It looks as if you have a new best friend,' I remarked as Teko knelt beside the wolf.

'I guess I do,' he said as he stroked the wolf's belly.

The meat was done and Teko divided it into three shares. And we all three ate wholeheartedly. It tasted like heaven in your mouth. The flavor was so strong we tried to savor every mouthful. I could never remember being this happy before. But I suddenly missed my grandmother. 'I know she is worried sick about me.'

Teko put his arm around my shoulders. Kissing me on the cheek. Don't worry you'll see her again soon. I will see to that. As the fire dwindled down, Teko felt me slip off to sleep on his shoulder. He closed his eyes while slipping into perfect peace under a beautiful starry night. As he felt himself slipping deeper into sleep, he could feel the wolf lying right at his feet. We awoke the next morning refreshed from a great night's sleep, regardless of sleeping from a sitting position. We had left over meat for breakfast before continuing onward.

It was mid-afternoon and we were walking along when I halted and drew in a deep breath and shuddered. I caught Teko's attention.

'You, OK?' he asked as he rushed to my side. He took my hand as I went down to my knees and cried.

Teko was getting worried, 'What's wrong Joan?'

Suddenly Teko sat back with a shocked look on his face. 'Oh, the gods have mercy. You felt him, didn't you?'

I regained myself with a lot of self will power.

'Yes, I felt him, it was only a brief second, but it was him. I know it was him. Oh, Teko we are getting close.'

'Are you OK to walk, or do you need more time to rest?'

'Oh no I am OK, Teko'

So, we walked on hand in hand. Just before dusk on the third night we saw the dim lights of the city on the horizon.

I think we should make camp here for the night. I don't feel safe camping close to the city. So, we made their camp near the river's edge. The stream had grown into a river. Almost without them noticing. It was such a gradual change. We heated some beans in a small pot for dinner and talked about our journey so far.

As we laid beside the fire in each other's arms with the wolf at their feet. I confessed, 'I can feel him stronger now. We are still a way away but getting closer. I can feel his energy pulling me in his direction. if that makes any sense.'

'Yes, it does, I can feel it too through you,' Teko said with a smile. 'Do you have an idea how we will get him back to the village?'

'Well, I can only hope to get close enough to fade into him. Once inside him I must persuade him into the woods.

Then we can tie him up and force him back with us.'

'That sounds as if it will work out great. You have planned this well, Joan.'

I laughed, 'I have just been following my heart.'

'Your great grandfather is the shaman, right?'

'Yes, I have never gotten to meet him.'

'You seem to have the abilities of a shaman.'

I gasped, 'I never thought of that. Wow that's crazy, but it does explain a lot of the things I can do.'

'Well,' Teko said, 'I think you are destined for greatness.'

Blushing I kissed him lightly on the mouth, 'If you are by my side.' With that I rolled over and was fast asleep. The next morning, I awoke early. Teko was still fast asleep. But the feeling he was closer woke her up. She stood and stretched.

The feeling came again this time it was stronger than ever before. I searched my mind and found a fox nearby. I faded into the fox and trotted off leaving Teko there to sleep I would just scout around and see what I can see. I had not gone more than a mile when I came upon a stable with several horses inside the barn yard. could feel their fear and see them stomp at the ground while the fox is close. So, I tried to stay far enough away as not to spook them too badly. Suddenly I came out on a walking trail of some sort.

The fox darted back into the edge of the underbrush where he cowered. Trembling in fear I tried to focus and see what was so bad. Suddenly the feeling of his energy was strong. Then I could smell him, his scent burned inside my nostrils, I could feel a fire raging inside of me. Burning deep in my soul. The smell of him was assaulting my very being.

Then he was there like a ghost appearing out of the morning mist. I could not believe what I was seeing. It was him there was no doubt at all. But this man was old, he staggered on a cane rather than walking. My heart was beating so fast with hatred for this man that the fox's heart nearly exploded under the pressure.

Suddenly I faded from the fox into him. When I slammed into him it was with such force, it knocked him right off his feet. He went sprawling face first onto the ground, breaking his nose and bursting both of his lips. As he sat up the blood was running from his nose and his lips, staining the white collar of his shirt.

Back at their camp, Teko slept while my body convulsed, my heart racing along with the memories rushing through me like a flooded river. What I needed to know most was in the forefront now. He lived in a retirement home, and he takes the long walks on the trails to get the tormenting thoughts out of his head of what he did to the Indian girl when he was in college.

My anger rose deeper. I wanted to slam his head into a rock, so his brains would splatter and feed the birds. But I knew in my heart he had to go back alive. So I persuaded him to go to the barn. There he saddled three of the horses. Once saddled, he mounted one and headed down the trail back toward the camp and Teko. My mind was racing a hundred miles an hour now.

I can't control my own damn mind. I cannot believe I have found the man I wanted. The man's mind seemed blank. As he sat atop the horse, I could feel his misery over what he did to my grandmother. But I could not bring myself to feel any pity for him. I hated him so bad.

As we got closer to the camp. I looked around for Teko. My heart leaped up into my chest when Teko stepped from the underbrush with his bow drawn back ready to shoot. I faded from the man back into my body. The sudden disappearance of me from him and the man was so startled that he fell from the horse. Teko reacted like a cat once the man hit the ground Teko was on him in the blink of an eye.

'No Teko,' I shouted as I approached them, 'we need him alive.'

Teko stared at me as his hand quivered with his knife against the man's throat. Ready for the kill. The man lay there on the ground trembling. Staring wide-eyed up at the two of them. He was speechless. He looked at them dumbfounded. Finally, he asked in low squeaky voice, 'What's going on here? How did I get out here?'

Teko shoved the knife blade harder into his neck. So hard I could see the thin line of blood that was oozing from around the edge of the knife blade.

'Easy, Teko,' I want nothing more than to see his throat slashed from ear to ear. But we need to take him back in one piece that way everyone will know the truth. We need to pack up and head back.'

'Head back?' the man croaked, 'Where are you taking me back to?'

'The Indian village of course, so you can pay for your crimes against my grandmother. And the village.'

The startled look of fear exploded in his eyes. There were instant tears streaming down his cheeks. Shaking his head after all these years of avoiding the Indian braves that came looking for him. 'I got caught by two children. I can't believe it.'

'Believe it,' Teko screamed into his face causing the man to recoil back. Teko brought the butt end of his knife down on the side of his head. The man's lights went dark. With the man being old and fragile it was not very hard to get his limp ragged body across the back of one the horses. Teko tied him tight to the horse.

'The horses are a welcome treat,' he said to me.

'Yes, we can make quick time heading back.' I then took my hands and cupped his soft cheeks. 'I could have never done this without you, Teko, and I thank you from the bottom of my heart.' I kissed him with pure passion.

'Anything for you,' he gulped out. 'Anything.'

Smiling we rode off at a fast gallop. Following the winding stream backwards, as we did coming down to this terrible place.

When we arrived back to where we had left the bear meat, we stopped to rest. I took the pot from the pack we had and went to get fresh water for us. As I was getting the water, Teko untied the man from the horse. Teko smiled as the man groaned from behind the rag around his mouth when his body got slammed to the ground as Teko jerked him from the horses back.

'You wait here,' he snapped. But before he turned to walk away, he gave the man a sharp kick to the gut. Making him ball up into the fetal position. After drinking his fill of fresh clean water, Teko took his large knife and began to cut large limbs to make a travois to take the massive bear carcass back to the village. The man sat and watched in stunned amazement. These two children had captured him with uncanny ease. They had also killed the largest bear he had ever seen. Who are these two anyway? They seem to work as one.

It was getting late in the afternoon when they had gotten everything loaded on the travois. When Teko suggested that they camp here for the night. I agreed, so Teko went after the firewood and I used the knife to cut a large chunk of the bear meat off.

Well, the old man's mind was whirling with thoughts. He did not want to die. Yet he knew if they took him back to the Indian village, that was sure to happen. So, in his mind he worked out a plan to wait till they fell asleep and he would make his escape. He sat there smiling to himself. He would be free soon. The twilight was deepening into darkness as the wonderful smell of the food cooking filled the air.

When Teko heard the rustling in the woods nearby the wolf stepped into the firelight. Teko and I smiled with joy at the sight of him but the man trembling with fear stumbled backward trying to fade into the tree. His eyes looked as if they would burst from their sockets. The wolf walked almost nose to nose with the man, he snarled showing his fangs. The drool was dripping from his muzzle.

'It's OK boy,' Teko spoke in his gentle voice. 'His remains will soon be yours.'

Before the wolf turned to walk away, he uttered a loud yelp blowing drool all over the man's face. Just then the man pissed himself. The wolf turned taking his front fore paw he scraped several paws full of dirt back at the man. The wolf walked over to Teko and I, there he sat down at our feet. When the meat had cooked, I offered the man a small piece, but he refused it, in his mind if he took the meat then the wolf would pounce upon him. Teko and I laid down on one side of the fire. Teko told the wolf to watch him. At this command, the wolf moved closer to the man and with every breath he took the wolf would open his mouth in a snarl. All the man's hopes of escape had shattered; all he could do was dwell on his upcoming death. He wished for it to be quick. It was barely daylight when Teko kicked the man in his ribs.

'On your feet scum,' he barked at him. They were all loaded up and ready to go. The man screamed in pain as Teko forced him over the back of the horse.

'Can I not ride upright for a change?' he grunted

'No, you will ride like a sack of shit you are.'

The man cried out in pain as Teko snatched the ropes tight binding him to the horse. I smiled at the sight of him in agony.

We headed for the village at the fastest pace we could pull the travois loaded with the bear meat. We travelled at a hard pace not stopping at all. At two o'clock Teko slowed his horse to a walk. I came up beside him and asked if there was something wrong.

'No, we are nearing the village. I know this area, I have hunted here before, after the first kill you helped with.'

'I only helped you.'

'I know, and I am glad you did,' and he gave her a warm smile.

Suddenly their hearts were pounding in their chests and when they reached the top of the rise in the trail the village came into sight.

I gasped, 'I hope to the gods that this works. If not, they will skin us both alive.'

'Never fear, Joan, I will be here for you. No matter what

happens.' He brought his horse next to hers, took her hand in his and kissed her lightly on her lips.

As we reached the edge of the village, we could hear a commotion happening. It was coming from the circle of the elders. Teko and I looked at each other.

'What's going on? I think it's about us.' Teko dropped his head. 'Yes, we are on the fourth day of travel now.'

Just before they turned the corner to enter the common area I whispered, I love you, Teko, thanks for everything.'

'I love you too, Joan.'

Then they were among all the villagers, who had stopped and were all staring wide-eyed at them. No one moved, no one made a sound. They rode up and dismounted before them. Teko took my hand and stepped forward. The four village elders and the shaman, Joan's great grandfather, emerged to the front of the crowd.

'What is going on with all this nonsense?'

The pair of them could see their family's eagerness to come forward but held their places. They both spoke in unison. We have brought the man back that has shamed this whole village.'

'The one that raped Joan's grandmother,' Teko spoke confidently like a man.

There was mumbling through the crowd. The chief of the village raised his staff high and suddenly there was silence. My heart was pounding in my chest. 'It's true Teko speaks the truth, now the whole village will know the truth about what happen that day to my grandmother. The lying rumors will now be put to rest.'

When my eyes met my grandmothers, I could see the trail of tears streaming down her cheeks.

Teko turned and snatched the old man from the horse. Stepping back as he thudded hard to the ground. Teko dragged him up before the elders. The man had tears in his eyes as he looks at my grandmother. It was as if he had seen a ghost. All he could manage was, 'I thought I had killed you with that rock to the head.'

In the next instant, the crowd gasped in shock. My grandmother was standing before him. Without a word she raised her hand above her head and brought it down swiftly. The knife she held in that hand suddenly slashed through the man's neck, severing his head from his body. As he fell, headless, to the ground at her feet, she spoke these words. 'You took my life and my daughter's life I now take yours.' At that she stepped back, and the rest of the villagers threw stones at the body till it was nothing but pulp. Just on the outskirts of the village the wolf stood drooling waiting on his opportunity to grab a piece of the man.

The End

THE CHRISTMAS SUPRIZE

It began on Christmas Eve, no one knew it was going to happen. When it did finally happen, it happened so fast it took everyone by surprise. Well, to be honest, it took everyone's breath away. It was your typical family Christmas get together. There were family members there that you only see once a year. Sometimes that once a year is even too much. All the adults were sitting around and conversing with each other. All the little children running around laughing and playing with their cousins. It was a joyous time. After everyone had eaten until they were full as ticks, the magic words the children were longing for was at last spoken. 'Time to open the gifts now.' The room erupted in shouts of joy. The children were running around madly. OK, one adult spoke up, settle down now. Get a seat so you can receive your gift. Slowly the kids reluctantly took a seat.

The excitement was building you could see it on everyone's face. Where's mine? I want a gift; that was the look you could see in their eyes. Heck even the little dog was excited, he has been here for the last four years, inside his little doggy brain, he knew he was going to get a new toy. Just then, as the first gift was to be passed out, the phone rang. The sudden loud ring broke the excitement, it also caused a little scream from a couple of the smaller girls.

'Merry Christmas,' our host, Cindy, said into the phone.

It was a one-sided conversation with us only hearing Cindy's side of the call. When she hung up the call the excitement in the room returned tenfold as Cindy announced that Josh and Tammy were on the way over and that they were bringing a game for everyone to play together to win a cool gift as a prize.

At last, the gifts were handed out. It was so joyous to see all the smiles on the faces of everyone as they opened their gifts. Sometimes it's not about what you get, it is all about the joy and fellowship with family. As things started to slow down, the little kids were occupied with their new toys. Most of the adults got fresh drinks. They began to talk about the game Josh and Tammy were bringing over. Some of them had played it before. So, they explained it to those that had never played before. There was a rumble to be heard over the noise. Could it be Santa Claus upon the roof, surely not. Jax let out a string of barks at the door. To loud cheers and shouts Josh and Tammy appeared in the doorway with two gifts in hand. We're here now so let the party begin. Everyone gathered around the table with only minimal pushing and shoving going on. Even little Jax the dog was under the table; he did not want to be left out.

Josh produced a large bag and he began to explain that there was a change to the game this year and he began to explain it like this. Josh reached into the large bag and pulled out a huge green Grinch's head. Several of the small kids jumped back in fright at the sight of the Grinch. Then they began to scream, 'Mommy look it's the Grinch he is here. Look Mommy.'

If you could only have heard the children, it was like they were chanting in surround sound. Once the laughter and excitement had died down some, Josh began.

'Here's the deal, we have two cool gifts here. Everyone will get a fair shot to win one of them or if you're lucky you win both. This is how you play. When it's your turn you will put the Grinch head on your head and then you put oven mitts on your hands and then try to open the gift. But there is a down side to it, as you are trying put your stuff on to open it the next player to your left is rolling a set of die, when they roll doubles then the players will switch out to the next player to the left. You will have to unwrap the gift, but you will also have to open the box to reveal the gift to receive it.' That is when the real fun began. With twelve people gathered around the table whooping and hollering. The laughter was deafening as we watched everyone try to unwrap a gift with oven mitts on their hands. Not to mention the huge Grinch head mask on so you could hardly see the gift you are trying to open. The first gift went around six times everyone had multiple chances to open it. When it was Tim's turn, he nearly had the gift box open when Cindy next to him rolled doubles, therefore she took the gift from Tim, it did not take Cindy long to get it open. Tim had done all the hard work right before her.

Cindy was thrilled she had won the prize. It contained two large candy bars along with a bag of candy and a computer cord. 'This is so cool,' Cindy shouted. She chanted, 'I am the winner.'

Tammy spoke up, 'Ah ha, I have another one we can play again.' There were yells and shouts of joy as the second round began. This round went much the same as the first round, there were many laughs as the gift was passed around from one to another. Allen was the lucky one this time around he got the gift unwrapped, there were shouts encouragement to hurry get it open. Some yelled, 'Hurry, roll doubles,' he just about got it open. Allen's heart was beating so fast in his mind he was repeating, I got this. Just as Allen removed the lid to the box, he heard the faintest sound of a click. That's when the whole world exploded into darkness.

PROLOG

No one had any idea what kind of monster Josh really was not even Tammy his wife of five years. Well, you see, Josh had built this massive bomb. It was to be sent to the governor's office on the first day of the new year. Instead of the bomb going to the governor, Josh managed to get the bomb mixed up with the gift to be wrapped for the party game. Our friend, Allen, was lucky enough to get it open. The explosion was so massive it destroyed an entire city block. It killed nearly three hundred people as they gathered in their homes with their families. I say nearly hundred only because we have no idea how many people the explosion vaporized into thin air.

The end

www.ingramcontent.com/pod-product-compliance
Lightning Source LLC
LaVergne TN
LVHW091933070526
838200LV00068B/957